Valen's Pack
Run with the Moon
Exodus

Coyote's Call
Off Course
In from the Cold
Blue Moon Rising

The Vamp for Me
My Life Without Garlic
Don't Stake My Life on It
Sunshine is Overrated
Don't Drink the Holy Water
The Trouble with Mirrors
That's One Cross Vamp

City Shifters
Bearly There
Harey Situation

Power
Exchange
Submit
Dominate

Mossy Glenn Ranch
Chaps and Hope
Ropes and Dreams
Saddles and Memories
Fences and Freedom
Riding and Regrets
Broncs and Bullies
Hay and Heartbreak
Vaqueros and Vigilance

Fire & Flutter
Dragon Dreams and Fairy Wings

Calendar Men

Mr. January
Mr. February
Mr. March
Mr. April
Mr. May
Mr. June
Mr. July
Mr. August
Mr September
Mr. October
Mr. November
Mr. December
The 13th Month

Fire & Flutter

Dragon Dreams and Fairy Wings

Wild Ones

Destined Prey

Anthologies

What's his Passion?: Unexpected Places
What's his Passion?: Unexpected Moments
Racing Hearts: The Lonely Ones

Love in Xxchange
Rory's Last Chance
Miles To Go
Bend
What Matters Most
Ex's and O's
A Bit of Me
A Bit of You
In My Arms Tonight
Where There's a Will
My Heart to Keep

Leopard's Spots
Levi
Oscar
Timothy
Isaiah
Gilbert
Esau
Sullivan
Wesley
Nischal
Justice
Sabin
Cliff

Mossy Glenn Ranch
Chaps and Hope
Ropes and Dreams
Saddles and Memories
Fences and Freedom
Riding and Regrets
Broncs and Bullies
Hay and Heartbreak
Vaqueros and Vigilance

Mystic Tattoos
One Too Many

Fire & Flutter

DRAGON DREAMS
AND FAIRY WINGS

BAILEY BRADFORD

Dragon Dreams and Fairy Wings
ISBN # 978-1-83943-953-7
©Copyright Bailey Bradford 2021
Cover Art by Erin Dameron-Hill ©Copyright January 2021
Interior text design by Claire Siemaszkiewicz
Pride Publishing

Published in 2021 by Pride Publishing, United Kingdom.

Pride Publishing is an imprint of Totally Entwined Group Limited.

DRAGON DREAMS AND FAIRY WINGS

Dedication

Keep reaching for the magic and love.

Chapter One

Blaze rubbed his shoulder where it still ached. He'd been lucky the whip had only caught him a glancing blow, otherwise he'd really be in pain.

Of course, even being whipped would be better than his punishment of not being allowed to fly. Or shift. Being stuck in the puny human form and dependent on two scrawny legs just sucked troll balls.

That imagery almost made Blaze gag. Trolls smelled *really* bad, worse than the dragon dumping grounds—and if anyone needed an explanation for what *that* area was, they didn't have a nose.

Plus, trolls were ugly. It was part of them being trolls and all. They also tended to have large, pendulous balls that swung down close to their ankles.

Blaze did gag then, pressing a hand against his stomach. He had to get his mind out of the troll gutter.

"Hey, freak, heard you got your powers taken away, all for a piece of ass."

Blaze glared at Bort. "Oh, yeah. Your dad wasn't worth it."

"My—" Bort's eyes glowed red, and smoke gusted from his nostrils. "I'll bake you, you fucking freak!"

Blaze kept his trembling inside. He'd learned not to show any fear to bullies. "Go ahead. King Fyre will be thrilled with you. You'll look great on a spit."

"You think just 'cause your brother's the king means..."

Blaze arched an eyebrow at Bort—which he knew looked cool, because he'd practiced it until he had it perfected and he knew how awesome that one arched eyebrow thing was. "It pretty much means he'll toast you if you lay a hand on me."

The only reason the guy who'd hit Blaze with a whip wasn't dead was because Blaze had kind of deserved it. Kind of, because he hadn't known Valdez was married to another man. Otherwise, Blaze wouldn't have fucked him. *Probably.* Blaze's morals were questionable at times, but only because he was so desperate for someone to touch him.

"Right, whatever," Bort drawled. "You'll probably cook yourself anyway and save all the good dragons the trouble. Crazy Blazy." He cackled and flipped Blaze off with both hands.

Probably with his toes, too, but Blaze didn't think to check. Instead he watched enviously as Bort shifted into a gorgeous teal and gold dragon.

Bort blew a stream of fire right past Blaze's head, then flapped his mighty wings and flew off. A rancid scent lingered in the air.

Blaze sighed and touched his hair that Bort had just singed. Everyone was going to think he'd done that to himself—again. Even though he was grounded, assumptions would be made that he'd done something stupid to burn his own hair, and rumors would fly. He'd have to worry about that later, if at all. Right now, he had to deal with a bully. Blaze really missed being able to shoot flames.

It was true that he couldn't control his fire, and he could be dangerous. He hadn't killed anyone on accident, yet, though. "Sheesh." Blaze sniffed and fanned the air around him. It was no use. The smell was on his head. He could fan all day, and it wouldn't make any difference.

Resigned to walking all the way back to his nest — which meant heading through the center of the dragon city, since he could no longer fly — Blaze prepared himself for the looks and murmurs. People would be talking about him more than usual today. He ought to be used to such stuff, but the truth was, it always hurt.

Even so, when he heard the buzz of conversations around him, Blaze held his head up high, despite the burnt hair. He hoped everyone gossiping about him got a snoot full of the noxious odor.

* * * *

"Where did I put my shoes?" Griff fluttered as much as a fairy without wings could as he looked for his soft purple shoes. Surprisingly, he could flutter a lot, although that translated into gestures with his hands and much twitching on his behalf.

"Did Egregio eat them?" Gia asked, hovering above him.

Griff glared at her. "Could you maybe not do that? I already feel like a complete loser without my wings." *Who knew they could be knocked off you?* Griff hadn't, and it'd come as a shock to the other fairies in his frolic. Of course, Love fairies weren't exactly brainiacs. They were more into the sensual than the mental. For brains, people looked to the Genius fairies, though good luck to anyone wanting help from those snobs. They didn't speak to anyone with an IQ under one-sixty—which left out most of the magic world.

"Sorry." Gia floated down and grimaced. "Ick. How can you tolerate standing all the time? My legs don't like it. It's *work*. It's so much easier to fly, or—" She smirked.

"Don't go there." Griff knew his own kind through and through. As a Love fairy, he shouldn't be bothered by hearing about his sister's sexual escapades. Maybe he was just jealous. "Keep your sordid stories to yourself."

Gia crossed her eyes at him. "Please. How did a prude get hatched into our frolic?"

"I've asked myself that a thousand times," Griff muttered. "Aha!"

"Aha what?"

Griff knelt and stuck his hand under his bed, then reached farther. "I swear to the gods, Egregio, if you bite me, I will feed you to the dragons."

"Rawr!" It sounded more like a whine than not.

Griff ducked his head and looked at the catterwaul under his bed. Much like the human-world cat except with two legs and large, hairy toes, and fangs the size of Griff's index fingers, the beast was rather fierce-looking.

"I'm not joking. Last time you bit me, it got infected. You're lucky I didn't toss you out then."

Beady red eyes glowed at him. "Rawr rawr rawr."

"Yeah, you're sorry now." Griff wiggled his fingers. "Give me my shoes."

The purple shoes were tossed at him while Egregio continued to vocalize.

"I know, I know, they're pretty. That's why I like them, too. Now if you're good, and you keep the dung beetles away for a whole week, I'll see about getting you your own shoes." Catterwauls were great to have as long as they were loyal. Sometimes they forgot that, though.

A few more *rawrs* and Griff was pretty sure he had his catterwaul vowing to fight off the shiny green beetles that migrated through the area on the way to the dragon dumping grounds. Griff hoped so. The buzz of beetle wings always left him with serious headaches as well as memories of the worst time in his life.

"Okay, got my shoes on, Gia. Now we can go…" Griff spun around, looking for his sister, but no. She had left the mushroom's interior at some point. "Great. Great! Now how am I going to find my way to where my wings might be?"

Griff couldn't remember things like he should have been able to. The hit he'd taken from a human's fly swatter had cracked his skull, knocked off his wings and almost killed him. His memory hadn't been right ever since, but he was lucky to even be alive.

Although the term lucky was relative. If he couldn't find his wings, what point would there be to life?

Chapter Two

After a month of being grounded, Blaze was desperate to be allowed to shift and fly again. *Very* desperate. Desperate enough to do something really icky if it'd get him out of trouble.

"I'll scrub the calluses off your feet—your paws," Blaze bartered, or tried to. His brother, aka King Fyre, seemed unimpressed with the offer. "Oh, come on, Fyre! You know how thick and callused your scales get back there! They turn all ashy and gr—"

King Fyre narrowed his eyes.

"—oss," Blaze finished, then gulped. "But in a kingly way. I mean that in a totally kingly, manly way."

Which was, apparently, the wrong thing to say, because Queen Bonny—short for Bonfire—threw her scepter at Blaze. "Ass!"

"Ouch!" Blaze yelped, not quite fast enough to avoid the heavy metal weapon. It *was* a weapon. Anything that hefty and pointy and well-aimed was definitely a weapon.

"Manly, you dork," Bonny snapped. "Like *that's* any proof of strength! You think having a dick makes someone strong?"

"No! Gods, no!" Blaze yelped again. He'd rather be hit with the scepter repeatedly than to hear Bonny talk about whatever she'd been about to say.

"What do you say?" Bonny purred, smiling evilly.

Blaze glanced at his brother. Yeah, he was getting no help there. Fyre was staring with utter adoration at Bonny.

Who growled at Blaze.

Blaze folded his stupid human arms over his stupid human chest. "Women rule and men drool."

"Say it like you mean it," Bonny demanded, but she giggled and winked at him. "It's so easy to get you riled up."

"You're the one who threw something," Blaze pointed out.

Bonny snorted, puffs of white smoke jetting from her nostrils. "Please. You threw stupid at me first."

Blaze wasn't sure what that even meant, so she was probably right.

"Your punishment remains in place," Fyre informed him, giving Blaze the stink eye. "There will be no escaping it this time. I've been entirely too lenient on you since our father and mother were eaten by the ogres. If they'd only listened to me…"

Blaze tuned his brother out. He had no memories of his parents. They'd died only a few weeks after he'd hatched, and he was lucky to have survived at all. It was commonly thought that his problems controlling his fire were due to the lack of a mother's love and milk. Bonny hadn't been around back then, and even if she had, she wasn't likely to have nursed him. She'd have thrown his rattle at him instead.

"Please," Blaze whined. "I hate being stuck in this body! It's awful! Puny and wobbly, and my—" Well, no. He wasn't going to go there. Of *course* his penis was smaller as a human. If it'd been the same size as when he was a dragon, he'd be all dick.

Blaze would have sworn by the gleam in Bonny's eyes that she'd heard his thoughts and believed he *was* all dick, just not the fun kind.

"There's nothing wrong with your human form, any more than there's anything wrong with mine, or Bonny's," Fyre said. "Are you implying *we* are flawed in these forms?"

Bonny picked up Fyre's scepter, which had a dagger-sharp tip.

Blaze wasn't stupid. "Nope. Nope. I'll just, er, I'll go pout in my room."

"No."

Blaze gawped at his brother.

"Close your mouth. You look like a moron," Bonny informed him.

Blaze snapped his mouth shut.

"No," Fyre repeated. "Your punishment isn't limited to you being unable to shift."

"It's not?" Blaze squeaked, his stomach dropping under the weight of dread that was suddenly on him. "Why not? I didn't know he was married, and everyone is usually scared to let me touch them. I just wanted—"

"I heard it the first time," Fyre said, holding up one hand in a gesture for silence. "And while I agree that he should have told you, there was still the wristlet. And the tattoo. It wasn't like he didn't have the ceremonial marital markings. The ink was still relatively fresh from those."

"He didn't remove his shirt!" Blaze tried once more to relieve himself of some of the responsibility. "He pulled down his pants, and waved his very bubbly butt at me—"

"Ew," Bonny interrupted, wrinkling her nose at him. "I would rethink your description there."

Blaze's cheeks heated, and he groaned as he covered his face with his hands. "Bonny!"

"Whatever happened, how it happened, the deed is done," Fyre said.

"Well, not really. *I* wasn't done," Blaze muttered.

This time he ducked just in time. The scepter sailed over his head.

"Regardless, if you bring this up to me again, I'll add another year to your punishment." Fyre waited.

Blaze bit his tongue to keep from saying something stupid. He wasn't opening his dumb human mouth this time.

Fyre nodded once. "Very good. As part of your punishment, you will be acting as guide to the fairy king, Artaxis, and his harem, while they are in this city. Whatever Artaxis requires of you, you will do it. I've had a room set up for you beside his. Be grateful I didn't put you beside the harem instead. Ninety-nine lovers— I can't imagine."

"You'd better not be trying to," Bonny warned. Too bad she was out of things to throw. She looked like she was considering removing Fyre's balls.

"Only you, my love," Fyre said with so much sincerity it was sickening. "I have need only of you."

Bonny sniffed and examined her talon-like nails.

Blaze didn't want to hang around with a bunch of fairies. "Why are they coming here?"

Fyre gave him a haughty look. "To work on the Dragon-Love fairy relations. Why else? We wish to forge an alliance in case the trolls and ogres join forces, as rumors have suggested they will."

"That'd be a nightmare," Blaze muttered.

"Exactly so, and we'd need allies. The Love fairies aren't just sexual beings. They're also very fierce fighters."

That made sense to Blaze. Surely Love fairies would have a lot of passion for most of what they did. Including killing.

"Fine. I'll do it." Blaze only sounded about ninety percent reluctant.

Fyre chuckled. "Boy, as if you ever had a choice in the matter."

* * * *

"There he is!"

Griff didn't recognize the speaker as he looked up to see a cloud of fairies above him. Way above him. One of them had on a crown so encrusted in jewels it should have weighed him down. It didn't.

"Griffwald! Your sister has been very worried," said the crown-wearing man.

Griff blinked at him.

The man floated down until he was closer to Griff. "Have you forgotten who I am?"

"I know who my sister is, and she's not you." That made sense, didn't it?

"I'm your king, Artaxis," the fairy said. "You were hurt. You forget things. Like your sister being a part of my harem." He pointed up.

Griff squinted. "Oh. Yes. I, um. Well. I was looking for my wings."

Artaxis sighed and placed a hand on his shoulder. "Griff, your accident occurred in an entirely different region. You were on your way to visit the Song fairies, to see if a young man there still held your interest. Do you remember that?"

"Now that you mention it—" Griff searched his memory. "No. But my wings aren't here?" He gestured around him.

"No, they are not," Artaxis said, his voice heavy with sadness. "I'm sorry, Griff. We looked for them, but I'm afraid they landed in the human realm, and…and they are probably gone for good."

Griff's eyes welled with tears, and his vision blurred. "No. I can't be a fairy without wings. I… I…" *What will I do?*

"Come with us." Artaxis slid an arm around his shoulders. "Get your mind off this for a little while. We're embarking on a grand adventure to visit the Fire dragons."

"Get my mind off of it," Griff muttered. "I'll forget again."

"Maybe it's not so bad to forget when something hurts you," Artaxis murmured. "Come. I'll have Lio go back to your 'shroom and stay with Egregio. Lio is terrified of the dragons and has been begging off this trip. Will Egregio eat him?"

"Probably not?" Griff wasn't certain.

"I'm sure Lio would rather risk the catterwaul than the dragons." Artaxis called over a dragonfly. "Here. Shadnay will happily give you a ride."

Well, it wasn't wings of his own, but the opportunity to fly was there, and Griff couldn't pass it up. "Thank you."

The dragonfly was an iridescent rainbow of colors, with fine, thin wings veined in gold. "Is it okay with you if I get on?" Griff asked. "Shadnay." He cautiously touched the silky-smooth creature's head. "Oh, you're blissfully soft and so warm! What a pleasure to touch you."

Shadnay buzzed at him and moved his wings out of the way.

Griff accepted that as permission to get on. He did so, careful not to hurt Shadnay, with the help of two of the harem members.

Then Shadnay rose into the air, and Griff lost himself in flight, in the beauty of the day and the magic of riding a dragonfly above the fields of flowers and grass.

Chapter Three

Blaze was as disappointed as all Hades. The fairies weren't little all the time. They were tiny when they came in, but quickly morphed to regular-sized beings, if not taller than most of the dragons when the dragons were in the two-legged form.

And holy dragon balls, Blaze did *not* know why *anyone* would want a harem! Okay, well, there was the sex, and lots of it, probably, but so far there'd been more bickering and outright fighting than anything sexy! He'd had to break up six altercations, and the fairies had only been in their accommodations for an hour!

This was going to be a long, suck-ass assignment.

The fairies sure were beautiful, though. Granted, he hadn't seen each and every one of them. He'd seen the king, and some of the harem members. Every one of them was gorgeous, delicate-featured, lithe and limber — that last one might not be true, but he was going to go with it, because...*hot! Bendy fairies...* Blaze adjusted his cock before it could pop up and embarrass him. He wondered if maybe, because they were Love fairies, they had special powers of attraction and such. He'd been fighting down boners ever since he'd been brought out to meet the Love fairy king, Artaxis.

Not that Artaxis even gave him a cursory glimpse. Blaze didn't blame him. Artaxis was beautiful, like all the fairies Blaze had seen so far, and Blaze was... Well, there was nothing delicate about a dragon's features, that was for sure. And lithe might apply to some of the other dragons in differing warrens, but not in any Blaze knew of.

Blaze had shocking orange hair and bronze skin...and freckles — another thing that was a burden to bear. How many times when he'd been a child had he been teased about having shit splatters on his face? Was it any wonder at *all* that he hated his human form? At least his scales made the freckles unnoticeable for the most part when he was a dragon. And Blaze was forever scarred from being told his freckles were caused by watching other creatures using the dragon dumping grounds. That was also the cause for styes in the eyes, according to old dragons' tales.

Blaze had never in his life had a sty, and he'd maybe, sorta accidentally, seen an orc once in the dumping grounds. If anything was going to give someone a sty, *that* should have done it.

Blaze smacked himself on the forehead. Why did his mind spin around to such stupid thoughts?

Well, it'd curbed his arousal. He hoped the fairies weren't going to hang around long. He didn't need the struggle with his dick, and he sure didn't need the blow to his ego — so far, none of the fairies had acknowledged him or even looked at him unless he was breaking up a fight involving them. Even then, he didn't think he registered as more than a big, lumbering weirdo.

He watched a dozen fairies walk toward the baths. They were so pale and pretty, and that long hair was amazing. Then he realized something wonderful. They were naked!

It was wonderful because there were so many gorgeous naked fairies. Yet it was horrible, too, because he was never going to have blood anywhere else but in his cock again unless he got some sort of control over his libido. When the fairies' hair swung just right, he saw glimpses of nicely rounded buttocks.

Blaze groaned and closed his eyes. He couldn't look. He'd end up taking his shaft out right there and jacking himself to completion, and he didn't have to think about it to know *that* wouldn't go over well with Fyre or Bonny.

He had to leave the hall next to the harem rooms, where he'd been standing, waiting for the next fight to break out. Blaze couldn't wait for more naked fairies to come out. He'd lose it and yeah, end up being grounded for a century.

It was easy to slip away, outside, into the heat of the sunlight. Blaze bit his lip until it hurt bad enough to kill his arousal. He was really going to have to get it together — if he could just figure out what *it* was.

A strange sound reached his ears. It was a fluttering, buzzing sound. He turned his head and frowned when he saw a gold-gilded dragonfly buzzing toward the entrance of the secondary palace where the fairies were staying.

Contrary to popular belief, dragons didn't look at dragonflies as cute little relatives. They looked at them as bugs.

Blaze raised a hand to swat it away when it was within reach.

* * * *

Griff was glad his sister had hung back with him. He'd been too nervous to meet the dragon king and queen. Shadnay had instead been kind enough to take Griff and Gia on a tour of his favorite meadow in the area. Filled with exquisite flowers in a multitude of colors, it brought peace to Griff and eased his soul, something he would never have expected. Even Gia had sighed and said she was glad she'd come along with him after all.

It'd been a blessing and such a respite from worry and stress. Griff had been happy, and finally was ready to join the other fairies.

And now there was a big orange idiot trying to swat him and Shadnay!

Gia shouted, and Shadnay vibrated with fear as he flew upward.

Griff had a horrible flashback—he was flying, singing merrily, full of hope that maybe the young man he was going to see would agree to being courted. Griff wanted someone, not a passel of lovers. He just wanted one that loved him. That made him a freak amongst his kind.

He'd been picturing the man's features—he couldn't quite make them out in the flashback, but something about them had given him hope—and singing, and flying. Then there'd been a shadow, one unlike anything in his world. It'd become incredibly cold, and fear had encompassed him. After that, he could only remember a *swoosh* and pain—

"Griff!"

It took him a moment to realize he was being shouted at. Griff sucked in a sharp breath and blinked until he could see the present rather than the past. Gia stared at him — big Gia, which meant she'd rearranged her size.

Griff might not remember everything he should, but he did remember how much he hated being small when Gia wasn't. He petted Shadnay on his silky head. "Thank you." Then he added a kiss, because Shadnay hadn't dumped him off or let him fall when Griff had been lost in that horrific episode.

Griff dismounted. Gia held him and Shadnay both in her palm. "Down, please."

She set him down, and Shadnay buzzed around, then shot straight up into the air.

Griff closed his eyes and concentrated. In a second, he was as tall as his sister. He looked into her lavender eyes, colored just like his own. "What happened?"

Gia patted his cheek. "Some dumb dragon drone tried to swat you and Shadnay. Don't worry. I put him down." She pointed.

Griff glanced at the prone form. Heat prickled along his spine as he took in the bronze skin and thickly muscled body. Long orange hair was splayed out around the man's head like a halo, or perhaps his own personal sun.

That bright hair was something. Griff's kind all had white hair, lavender eyes and pale, pale skin. This man was nothing like them, with his broad features and amazing coloring.

"Wipe the drool off your chin, brother mine," Gia sang. "He's an idiot and would have killed you and Shadnay without a thought. Makes him a brute as well."

Griff sighed and looked away from the man only to return his gaze again. *He has freckles!* Over his cheeks and the bridge of his nose. There were even some on his chest that Griff could see thanks to the opening of his shirt.

But it didn't matter how cute those freckles were, or how intense a contrast they were to the man's bulk, or how much his hair looked like the rising sun. He'd tried to kill Griff unthinkingly.

"He'll wake up when the spell wears off," Gia said. "Come on. I'm going to have to fight for my place in the harem. It's my night to be with Artaxis. I'm third, and that's a good place to be. He lasts longer and gives more foreplay once he's fucked a couple of us first."

Griff moaned and covered his ears. He turned away from the sun-man and glared at Gia. "I don't want to hear such things."

She tittered. "Made you stop staring at that jerk."

Shadnay landed on his shoulder after Griff lowered his hands. If he peeked back at the downed man, no one but him and Shadnay had to ever know.

Chapter Four

Blaze's head was still pounding hours after he woke up on the ground. The last thing he remembered was a dragonfly, then his brain must have swelled and tried to escape his skull.

Then again, he did have a knot the size of a dragon 'nad on the back of his head. What he couldn't figure out was how he'd ended up on the ground in the first place.

Maybe the dragonfly tripped me. Those little buggers were fierce! And tricky. *And trippy.* He groaned and covered his face with his hands. Even alone, he was ashamed of that joke. It was no wonder he was single.

He tossed in his bed. It was a comfortable mattress and all, but he was just befuddled by the whole afternoon. The more he thought about it, the more he thought maybe he'd heard a shriek — one like a pissed-off harpy was coming at him — right before he'd lost consciousness.

What does that mean? Blaze didn't know.

Despite the thick walls between his room and the harem room—which was really a series of several rooms converted into a huge area for the fairy king's visit—loud moans penetrated the wall.

Blaze snickered. There was definitely some penetrating going on.

Except not for him. "Damn it." He was torn between listening intently and banging on the wall. Since banging on the wall would no doubt be considered rude of him, he settled for listening.

Then he felt like a dirty dragon, and he covered his head with both of his pillows. When he couldn't breathe, he lifted the edge of the pillow and pursed his lips.

He'd have sworn the sounds from the harem room got even louder. *Squealing zealots! What* are *they doing in there?* He'd never had sex that resulted in that much noise! Maybe he was doing something wrong.

Blaze tentatively pushed the pillows up. Was that a violent thump he heard? He should probably just go take a peek and make sure no one was getting beaten—unwillingly—in the harem room.

It *could* have been a groan of pain, not a moan of pleasure.

Right? Right. He should go check. Just open the door and take a quick look. It was part of his punishment, after all. He couldn't allow someone to get hurt. And as many fights as there'd been over there, well...

Blaze tossed the pillows aside. He glared at his half-hard dick, tenting his sleep trousers. "Stop it, or I won't play with you."

Lies, all lies! I'll be playing with you the second I finish looking into that room. Possibly sooner, depending on what he saw.

All in the name of doing his appointed punishment, of course.

Blaze got up out of bed when the doorknob started turning.

"What the—" he whispered, eyes wide and heart slamming. What kind of magic was that?

He supposed someone could be coming to talk to him, but his mind blanked over who. The king would have sent a guard, who would have knocked, and no one had knocked.

The knob continued to turn, and Blaze dropped back onto his bed for reasons he couldn't explain. He tried to stay out of sight, then when the door opened slowly, anticipation made his skin prickle.

One slim, finely shaped bare foot appeared, the skin so pale it almost glowed. He'd never seen such a fine-boned ankle before. Dragons were stocky and thick, though they did *not* have cankles no matter what those stupid minotaurs claimed. Minotaurs were assholes anyway.

Not a single hair marred the smooth skin on the leanly muscled calf that appeared next. Blaze held his breath, watching eagerly, no longer worried about who was sneaking into his room.

His cock was fully hard by the time he saw the naked thigh, but he was disappointed when the hint of clothing appeared in the form of a short, flowing hemline.

The green material looked to be as soft as the man's skin. Blaze licked his lips and waited for more, but instead got a gasp and a squeak.

He jerked his gaze up and found himself staring into the prettiest purple eyes he'd ever seen. So wide they shouldn't have been possible on a living creature and uptilted beautifully at the outer edges. Dark purple ringed the lighter irises, with flecks of silver mixed into the lavender.

The pert, thin nose and lush pink lips just about did Blaze in. He pressed a hand to his throbbing cock and wondered what he'd have to do to get those lips around it.

"I'm—I'm s-sorry," the fairy stuttered, the pale skin of his cheeks darkening to pink. "I-I was l-looking for s-someone else."

Blaze crooked a finger at the fairy. "But you found *me*, so why don't you come in?"

Griff knew Gia was somewhere. He just…didn't know where. He'd come along on a trip when he shouldn't have. His sense of disorientation was troublesome. All he wanted was to go back home.

And instead, he found himself in the room of the orange-haired man Gia had knocked out hours ago.

Going into the room with the man was stupid. He probably wanted to squash Griff flat for Gia's spell. Then again, he might not remember it. Gia had said he wouldn't.

But Griff remembered the man trying to kill him.

"N-no. You tried to k-kill me," he accused, yet he didn't back away. He'd seen the man push down on his erection. For some reason, that move held Griff in place.

The dragon scowled. "I did not! I wouldn't try to kill an attractive man. Or even a moderately not ugly man. I can't be picky here."

"What?" Griff's fear was trampled by confusion. "What are you going on about?"

The dragon snorted and rolled his eyes. "Oh please. Look at me. Do you think I have handsome men sneaking into my room all the time? Or often? Or ever?"

Griff hated to break it to him, but— "I was looking for my sister. And you *did* try to kill me earlier, and my friend Shadnay, who'd been nice enough to give me a ride to the palace."

"I am so confused."

Griff pushed the door open a little wider. Maybe if he didn't go in, he'd be safe enough talking to the intriguing, but possibly psychotic, dragon.

"I was on Shadnay the dragonfly, and you tried to squish us," Griff explained slowly, in case the other man was a bit thick in the head. He didn't know dragons, or whether low intelligence was common for them.

"Dragonfly?" The man's entire expression turned to one of horror. "Dragonfly! Oh shit!"

Griff cringed at the curse word and covered his ears.

"Sorry!" The dragon scrambled off the bed. If he'd had an erection earlier, it was gone now.

"Sorry, oh gods and spawns, I didn't even—" He gulped, then turned an unattractive shade of green. "Uh. What if I've squished other people? I'm going to be sick!"

He ran for a door across his room.

Griff stood there, hesitant to help yet not wanting to leave. He should have been terrified.

Instead, he was struggling not to be intrigued. He didn't like violence, and he'd seen proof already that this particular man reacted with violence first and thought... Well, who knew when he ever thought?

Yet Griff remained in place, waiting for his return.

31

Chapter Five

It was strange. Griff had trouble remembering the oddest things — like who his king was — but he'd remembered the orange dragon without any trouble at all. Maybe it was the man's unusual coloring, or those divine freckles.

Griff cringed when he heard another gut-wrenching sound. He was fairly certain he hadn't almost been murdered on purpose earlier. That still didn't stop his mind from flitting around the dark edges of something he didn't care to remember.

"I'm so, so sorry," the dragon said before he'd even come out of the bathroom. "I didn't think — I mean, I've only seen fairies that are, you know, not little. Well, you aren't exactly big like we are, kinda delicate-looking —"

Griff stuck his tongue out even though he couldn't be seen. He heard water running then the sound of gargling. He twirled a few strands of hair around one finger. *Delicate-looking. He didn't say delicate. He might think we are, though. Should I be offended or not?* Considering he wasn't certain the man was all that intelligent—dragons as a whole might be more brute than brains, for all he knew—Griff decided to go with not being offended. It took up too much energy to be pissy.

But he could make a point. "So a delicate female fairy kicked your behind earlier today."

"What?" the dragon bellowed. It sounded like he sputtered and spat his gargling liquid all over the mirror. The water was shut off as the man coughed and hacked. "A *girl?*" he finally got out, appearing in the bathroom doorway, face red, eyes bloodshot, and drool on his chin. He took off his shirt, which was also wet, and exposed Griff to honey-gold skin dusted with freckles and orange hair.

"I think I'm in lust," Griff muttered, eyeing pretty coral nipples. *Now* he understood what his kind of fairy was supposed to be doing. He wanted to jump on the dragon and ride until they were both limp and sated.

Except there was that whole comment about a girl, and Griff really didn't like people who thought less of women than men. "No, a woman," he stressed, narrowing his eyes at the dragon. Griff's fingertips buzzed and tingled, and little bolts of iced-energy zipped from the tips. He didn't lose control, though it was tempting to zap the dragon.

But the dragon held up his hands. "What? Hey, no, no, I didn't mean anything bad by it! Don't glare—it makes my head ache! And our women—girls included—are fierce and deadlier than the males! Nothing but respect for the fiercer sex!"

As far as backpedaling went, that was pretty good. "Well, you just—" Griff began, only to be interrupted.

"It's just that all of you fairies look like you'd break easy," the dragon said, obviously not seeing the danger in letting his tongue overrule his brain.

Then again, maybe there wasn't any danger, Griff reminded himself.

Griff sighed. Maybe dragons were dense and only understood one thing. If that was the case, then he could straighten out this particular dragon very quickly. "What's your name?" he asked. "I'm Griff."

The dragon lowered his hands and smiled rather charmingly, if naively. "Griff, huh? That's a wicked cool name. I'm Blaze, on account of me being part of the royal family. We get the hot names, you know, like Fyre and Bonfire and, well, Blaze." He preened, sticking his admittedly nicely stacked chest out. The smile was on the cheesy side, but Griff was strangely charmed.

And rethinking the whole, *setting the dragon straight* thing. He didn't want to start a dragon-fairy war by offending anyone.

But...he wouldn't do permanent damage, and it might do the dragons good to learn that fairies weren't helpless.

Griff felt a stirring of excitement unlike anything he could remember experiencing — which wasn't saying too much, considering his memory stank. Still, his grin might have held a little fairy impetuousness to it.

That smirk was a forewarning, Blaze was sure of it. He just didn't know *what* the bad thing was that was going to happen. Blaze wrapped his hands around the back of his head. "Not again!"

Griff blinked in a slow way that was sensuous and pretty all at once. "Not again?" he questioned.

Blaze nodded. His head throbbed. "Ow. Ow! Yes, no."

"You're making absolutely no sense," Griff said, doing the blinky thing. "None."

Blaze thought about what he'd just said. "Oh. Well, I mean…er. My head hurts, so the ow. Then I nodded so another ow, because, um. Ow?"

Griff arched one thin, already pretty damned arched eyebrow.

Blaze wasn't sure if he was blushing or if his powers were fixing to go haywire on him. "Um. The, uh. Yes, I meant not again, but no, I didn't mean yes, *do* it again." *Ugh!* Could he sound any dumber?

Hm. Probably.

Griff pursed his lips, making them into a very lovely *o*.

Blaze wanted to lick them. Suck them, maybe, and test their lushness with his teeth. Feel them on his skin and —

But Griff spoke and kind of cracked that spell holding Blaze in a stupor over those lips.

"Ah, I didn't think about the backatcha spell Gia flung at you," Griff murmured. "You're lucky she held back, or you'd have been as splattered as you intended me and Shadnay to be."

"The backatcha —" Blaze let go of his own noggin.

"Yes, that particular spell takes whatever you were about to do and throws it back at you," Griff explained patiently. "Gia is one of the more powerful fairies in our frolic."

Blaze might have giggled. "A frolic?"

"Did you just…" Griff took a step toward him, something like wonder in his voice. "Giggle?"

Blaze slapped a hand over his mouth. "Noophth."

"You did!" Griff squealed, but it wasn't like the annoying, eardrum-piercing squeals coming from the harem room. It was throaty and hot, and Blaze's stupid dick was going to spring up and bob for attention.

"You giggled, and it was adorable," Griff continued, taking another step closer. "And I remember you, and why I'm here in this room. I was looking for my sister, but instead, I found the golden dragon!"

Now, Blaze was hardly golden. He was orange. He knew it, and every dragon in the damn clutch knew it.

But Griff was looking at him like he was truly special, and not in that snarky joke special way that he'd heard so often when he'd been growing up. And just earlier that day.

No. Griff was looking at him like Blaze was... interesting, and not a freak.

Blaze gulped. He didn't know what to say or do and he didn't want to move or speak and screw it all up. He really liked the way Griff was staring at him, the warmth in the fairy's eyes and the way those lush lips parted on a big smile.

"What are you doing in here with *him*?" shrieked someone who was definitely *not* Griff.

Griff spun around, and Blaze guessed it was a fairy version of a blush that tinted every bit of Griff's skin the same lavender as his eyes. "I-I-I-I—"

A female fairy flitted into the room, glaring daggers at Blaze. "I should have zapped your ginger ass harder!"

"Gia!" Griff covered his ears. "Language!"

Gia rolled her eyes. "Get over your delicate sensibilities, brother! And get out of this nutjob's room. Come on. You got lost again, didn't you?" She took Griff by one hand. "I've already had my fun in the harem. Let me get you to your room, and don't leave again until I come for you in the morning. Not that you'll remember I said so. I'll have to write a reminder spell—"

"I wasn't lost," Griff whispered, turning his head to look at Blaze. "Not this time."

But Blaze didn't know what had happened or why Griff was letting himself be dragged away, especially not when he'd been eyeing Blaze so thoroughly.

Was it another rejection? And why wouldn't Griff remember what his sister said?

And worst of all, why had Griff sounded as lost as his sister said he was when he'd let himself be led away?

Chapter Six

Despite all the racket coming from the harem room, Blaze did eventually manage to fall asleep. Of course, his dreams were filled with a sexy male fairy. Blaze enjoyed the first couple of those dreams. He woke up from the second one with a raging hard-on he couldn't ignore.

Blaze reached under the thin sheet covering him. His sleep pants were a pain to get open, but the second he did, he spat on his palm. Blaze gripped his cock and started jacking off. Normally he liked to take his time to work up to his climax. But he was already so close that he couldn't go slow. He stroked his shaft rapidly, roughly, chasing a burn and twist of pleasure.

In an embarrassingly short period of time, he jerked from head to toes. His abs went taut, and his breath rushed from his lungs. He couldn't keep back a growl as he came, images of lavender eyes and long white hair so clear in his mind. Pale, soft skin—it'd feel like nothing he'd ever touched before, so perfect, smooth, warm.

Blaze practically swallowed his tongue as his climax ripped through him, all but turning him inside out. He'd come so damn quickly, he hadn't even gotten to fantasize. He'd just had those flashes, and they'd sent him skyrocketing into orgasm.

It wasn't unusual for Blaze to develop crushes on guys he didn't know. It was easier, actually. Safer. Well, usually, not counting the fuckup that had ended with him being grounded.

Although, to be fair, he hadn't had a crush on Valdez.

Blaze sighed and wiped his hand on the sheet. He used another part of it to clean off his cock and belly, then tossed the material on the floor and tried to go back to sleep.

His dream, when he did, wasn't steamy this time. Not at all. Blaze woke up, sweating, heart slamming, a shout ringing in his ears, throat aching. He couldn't stop seeing it—his hand swatting at an annoying dragonfly, not missing this time. And knowing he'd killed Griff.

It wasn't real. It hadn't happened. Griff was fine.

But that nightmare kept Blaze from getting any more rest.

* * * *

Gia had been annoyingly overprotective earlier. Griff didn't know what had crawled up her butt. Maybe it was the fact that he'd almost gotten killed. He could never tell with his sister.

Griff looked around the room he'd been put in. It was fancy-schmancy, with gold-framed paintings and drapes that probably cost a fortune. The furniture was all icky.

Heavy, dark, so masculine it'd cause anyone sleeping in there for more than a week to grow a pair of balls.

Griff hardly had need of the one pair he had. What would he do with two?

He glared at the bed. He knew exactly where he was, and why. His memory was being his friend right now.

In fact, all his body felt pretty good for once. He missed his wings but flying on Shadnay had given him a measure of peace he'd been missing. It wasn't a permanent fix—it'd just lifted his spirits.

And that dragon, Blaze, he'd lifted something else of Griff's. Something considerably lower down than where a fairy's soul resided.

Griff giggled and noted the way his genitals were only barely covered by the material he wore. He'd never been one for easy sex once he'd tried it a few dozen times, but he was certainly considering making an exception for Blaze. Weird that he was so attracted to a guy who'd almost killed him.

It *had* been an accident, though.

Maybe it'd been an accident that had cost Griff his wings, too.

Well, *that* totally dampened Griff's arousal.

"Oh no." He fluttered one hand in front of him before resting it over his heart. "What if I'm attracted to men who want to kill me?" Would he get an erection if he saw the human who'd hurt him so badly?

Dang it. His head was still a mess even if his memory was functioning for once. He was being paranoid, wasn't he?

Aren't I? Griff racked his brain trying to recall who'd swatted him so severely. He couldn't picture him, not even a hint of him. Yet Griff knew without a doubt it'd been a man.

Oh, it was a puzzle, all right. Griff thought it over all night and into the first hour of the morning.

It was worth it. At least he figured out that he hadn't been feeling horny when he'd gotten hit. That had to mean something good.

And he was fascinated with the dragon for reasons he couldn't pin down. The freckles were part of it, but only part.

One thing he did know, he was going to see the dragon again, soon. Griff ran over to the window. He traced a map onto its surface, hoping it'd still be there in case he forgot how to get to Blaze's room.

Chapter Seven

"Mother of pearl! Ugh!" Blaze pulled the pillow over his head. "What in all of Hades are you fairies *doing?*" he shouted.

"Each other!" several musical-tinged voices hollered back, along with a chorus of titters and giggles Blaze heard through the stupid wall.

He thumped his head against the mattress. The knot he'd had from being knocked on his ass was gone, but he still winced as slippery little tendrils of pain wrapped around his skull. Apparently the area was tender.

Blaze tried sticking his fingers in his ears. That helped some, until his ears started to ache. It didn't help that every time there was a moan or shout or garbled whatever-it-was sound of release, he wondered if it'd come from Griff.

It stood to reason that Griff was part of the harem. The king had arrived with his lovers, and as far as Blaze knew, that was it. So that meant Griff was one of the fuckers or fuckees — or both, or who knew what — next door.

Every time Blaze thought of that, he growled, and had he been able to, he'd have shifted and toasted some fairy asses. So it was probably a good thing he couldn't shift. He didn't think he'd kill anyone, but then again, as unreasonable as he was feeling about Griff having sex with others, who knew? Obviously, Blaze was losing his mind.

He didn't know Griff. He'd tried to *kill* Griff, for goodness' sake! Griff certainly wouldn't be interested in him in any manner except possibly as a target for retribution. Even though Blaze hadn't ever intended to hurt Griff, he'd been stupid and careless and inattentive, and he could have done such a horrible thing.

Blaze stiffened. Now the fairies were doing something that resulted in a very annoying banging sound. That was it. He was going to go beg Bonny to move him to the other end of the castle tomorrow. He'd prostrate himself if necessary.

The banging grew louder. Blaze threw the pillow on the floor and sat up, mouth open to shout. Then it occurred to him that someone was knocking on his door, not the wall. "Oh. Oops." *Now who'd be coming to my room at this time of night?* He hoped it wasn't that pissed-off sister of Griff's, who'd been by the night before, dragging Griff away from him.

Blaze's skin tingled with anticipation as he got up and crossed the room. An odd, warm sensation filled him when he reached for the door.

Maybe he was getting sick. At least he could sprint to the toilet quickly if he needed to.

Blaze opened the door and blinked, his cock instantly perking up as he stared at Griff. "Uh?"

Griff blinked back at him, those pale cheeks turning pink.

Blaze really, *really* liked the way Griff looked when he blushed. Griff's lips were parted, too, and he licked the bottom one. Blaze hoped he only whimpered in his own head. He was supposed to be a big butch guy and whimpering was kinda contrary to that as far as he knew.

Except this look came over Griff, a sultry, sexy expression carrying enough heat to make any dragon proud.

Blaze wasn't usually so bold. He normally took what was offered, didn't reach for what he wanted. He'd been shot down too many times to dare take a chance.

And yet, he opened the door wider, took a step back while at the same time cupping Griff's elbow, pulling him into the room.

Griff came willingly, almost predatorily, in fact. Blaze shut the door.

It hadn't taken a map to guide Griff back to the dragon. All he'd had to do was listen to an instinct he couldn't name.

And now he was finally there, with the dragon— *Blaze.* He even remembered Blaze's name.

In fact, Griff thought he remembered everything about Blaze, though he supposed, with his mind, that might not be true. Still, he was here now, and he wanted Blaze. Craved him like crazy.

The Love fairy part of him was in full effect. Need filled him, empowered him, pulsing throughout his body like the blood pumping through his veins.

He liked the whimpering sounds Blaze made, liked the wide-eyed want, the eager, nervous way Blaze was moving backward, the grip Blaze had on his arm.

Griff, who'd felt so powerless for so long without his wings, was powerless no more. He walked Blaze backward to the bed, hardly feeling the floor beneath his feet.

"I—" Blaze stuttered, then gasped when the backs of his legs hit the bed.

Griff delighted in everything about Blaze in that moment. The shock, lust, nervous twitching, and the thick, hard ridge of the cock tenting Blaze's pajama bottoms.

Griff pulled his elbow free and ran his hands over Blaze's bare chest. The freckles all over it needed to be tasted. He pushed and sent Blaze sprawling onto the bed.

"Whoa!" Blaze grunted and caught himself on his elbows before scooting around to prop himself against the headboard.

Griff couldn't remember ever wanting anyone so bad, not even the man he'd been going to see before his accident. Griff couldn't remember that man at all. He only had other people's word on that. For now, anyway. Later he might remember more.

Now he wanted to concentrate on the big golden man licking his lips and palming his erection.

Griff wanted to touch and play and fuck.

But more, he wanted to kiss Blaze and explore the vast expanse of skin.

"I want—" Blaze began.

Griff removed his covering, letting the silken material slide to the floor.

Blaze gasped and shoved his pajama bottoms down, his gaze darting all over Griff's nude form.

The open appreciation was making Griff's cock harder than ever. If he wasn't careful, he'd end up spilling his seed in a short period of time. He didn't want to shame his kind. Love fairies were made for loving, for sex and magic and beauty.

And he was going to give every one of those things to Blaze. Something about the dragon touched Griff. There was a vulnerability to Blaze that Griff had caught a glimpse of, and oddly enough, that made the man sexier than someone perfect and full of himself.

Griff moved closer, then climbed onto the bed. He placed a hand on Blaze's knee. "Where to start?" he wondered out loud.

Blaze leaned forward. "I—with a kiss?"

That seemed like a brilliant idea to Griff.

Chapter Eight

Blaze had never felt so aroused. The deep core of fire in him was raging, and it was a wonder he wasn't shooting flames from his fingertips. He watched hungrily as Griff, so gloriously nude and perfectly sculpted, climbed onto the bed to straddle him.

There was so much pale, smooth skin to touch! Blaze hesitated, hands hovering before he finally reached for Griff's chest, drawn to the tiny pink nipples there.

The instant his palms pressed to Griff's skin, Blaze gasped, the heat inside him flaring brighter.

Griff gasped as well then bent and slanted his mouth over Blaze's.

Never had Blaze been kissed with such sweet, hot intent. He'd had sloppy, do it 'cause he was fucking kisses, but nothing like how Griff was kissing him. Gentle yet insistent, careful, as if Griff were savoring the taste of Blaze.

Blaze shivered and curled his fingers as Griff's tongue slicked over his.

Griff's breath hitched, and those tiny little nubs went hard beneath Blaze's hands.

Someone has sensitive nipples, Blaze thought, before Griff shattered his ability to think by deepening the kiss.

Griff cupped Blaze's jaw and used his other hand to stroke Blaze's hair. Everything felt so good, Blaze couldn't tell where the pleasure began or ended. Maybe it didn't. Maybe that sensuous enjoyment was a vital part of him in that moment.

He pressed his hands against Griff's nipples, rubbing them, stimulating his fairy.

Griff kissed him with an edge of desperation. He nipped at Blaze's lips, at his tongue, and ran his fingers over Blaze's scalp, making him purr. No one had ever done half the things Griff was doing to him, and they'd only just started.

There'd be nothing left of himself when Griff was done with him. Blaze would melt from the rapturous feelings Griff was filling him with.

Griff used his grip on Blaze to turn Blaze's head to the side.

Blaze sucked in a great big breath, dizzy from the lack of enough oxygen.

Then Griff began sucking on his neck, and Blaze made an odd, warbling sound. He slid his hands around to Griff's back, holding on for all he was worth. The slight weight of the fairy belied the strength in his body. Blaze felt the muscles under that smooth, warm skin. Griff was lean and strong and soft and —

"Ungh!" Blaze jerked, his toes curling as he thrust his hips. He felt Griff's long, pale shaft that he'd seen moments before. The soft press of Griff's balls was a welcome weight as Griff began to frot against Blaze.

Blaze wasn't going to last. He zipped his hands down to cup two sumptuous ass cheeks. They fit so perfectly in his grip, and the warmer skin between them drew Blaze's fingers like a beacon guiding them home.

As he thrust up again and again, Blaze forgot to censor his whimpers and needy sounds. His eyes rolled when Griff bit and sucked on his neck. There'd be marks — Gods, he hoped there'd be marks!

Griff undulated and drove his rigid cock against Blaze until Blaze was right at the peak, right about to tumble over into what would no doubt be the best orgasm of his life.

And Griff stopped moving those slender hips.

What should have been "*Griff*" came out more like a bad mix of consonants having nothing at all in common with any letter in the fairy's name.

Griff chuckled against the wet, sensitive skin of Blaze's neck. The sound was darkly enchanting. "Oh, dragon-mine," Griff said, every word digging a deeper well of desire into Blaze. "Don't you know? I'm a Love fairy. I'm going to blow your mind, all night long."

Blaze whimpered again.

Griff hadn't wanted anyone in so long, and never like he wanted Blaze. It was important that he bring as much pleasure to the dragon as he possibly could. He had to impress himself on Blaze — the need to ensure that Blaze would want him again was overpowering and Griff didn't have the strength, or any good reason he could think of, to fight it.

But imprinting on someone, that was a big thing for a fairy, any fairy, whatever their breed. Imprinting meant belonging to that one person, just *one*. It didn't occur to Griff that was what he was doing until he pulled Blaze back from the sensual edge a fourth time. *Imprinting! Gods! Am I really?*

And he couldn't force himself on Blaze, whom he didn't know, couldn't tie himself to one man during their first sexual encounter together. That was unheard of and foolhardy, and Griff just managed to get a grip on his instincts before he could murmur the binding words for them.

It shook Griff to his soul, both the almost-binding and the part where he forced himself to stop. He wouldn't deny either of them relief, however. They both deserved to be awash in ecstasy.

So Griff bit his tongue and took one last look at the marks he'd left on Blaze, then licked a path down Blaze's body, to the fat tip of his cock.

Dragons' penises were a little different from fairies', and possibly from any other kind. There were ridges circling the length of that thick cock, smooth, rounded ridges that would feel incredible inside a man's ass.

Griff was going to find out how they felt in his mouth. He licked over the leaking slit and gripped the base. At the same time, he used his other hand to stroke his own dick.

Blaze's pre-cum tasted hot and spicy, earthy and strong. Griff hummed and sealed his lips over the entire tip. Then he sucked.

"Argh!" Blaze grabbed Griff's head.

Griff expected him to try to take over, but he didn't, much to Griff's delight. Blaze merely left his hands in Griff's hair, and waited, squirming against the bed a little.

Griff rewarded him by taking as much of that thick length into his mouth as he could. The cap was broad enough to make deep-throating a serious challenge, and it took Griff a couple of attempts before he got it in that far. When he did, and he swallowed, Blaze bellowed loud enough to shake the walls.

Griff bobbed up and went after the little bundle of nerves beneath the cap. He left off jacking himself to instead shove that hand under Blaze's butt.

He went right for Blaze's hole, burying his thumb between Blaze's cheeks and rubbing, pushing at that tight entrance. When the tip eased in, Blaze's ring gripped it so tight that Griff's thumb tingled.

He dove back down on Blaze's cock, flicking his tongue over every ridge. He couldn't get all Blaze's shaft in his mouth — it was simply too big, although there was nothing simple about it, really.

But Blaze was obviously loving what was happening. He panted and writhed, shouted and pleaded — either to come or for Griff to draw out the pleasure longer, Griff wasn't sure which.

Griff pushed more of his thumb into Blaze's hole and swallowed around the tip of Blaze's cock. He rotated his thumb, then swallowed again.

Blaze's bellow was incredible. So was the tight, tight grip of his ass and the hot jet of spunk that poured down Griff's throat.

Griff pulled back and caught the rest on his tongue. It was spicy, like Blaze's pre-cum, but with a surprisingly sweet flavor to it as well. Griff could quickly become addicted to the taste of it.

He pulled off and caught the last spurt in his hand. Griff kissed the tip of Blaze's cock then, before easing his thumb from Blaze's hole.

Blaze moaned, and Griff scrambled up to straddle Blaze's hips again. He planted his butt right on top of

Blaze's cock and writhed, driving more wanton sounds from the dragon.

Griff used Blaze's cum for lube, spreading it on his own aching length and moaned, while Blaze gripped Griff's thighs and rutted against Griff's ass. Griff palmed his balls as he jacked off, his breath short, his need great.

Blaze opened his eyes, and the fiery look he shot Griff sent him spiraling into orgasm. Griff threw his head back, and a sound like a song left him as he spilled his seed on Blaze's chest.

They almost escaped from him, those magic words of promise and forever. Griff bit his tongue until he tasted blood. It was the only way he could keep the last sentence unspoken and from allowing the imprinting to enter into a state of permanence.

Even with the imprinting denied, the orgasm was intense. Colors swirled before Griff's eyes — the violet and white twined with pinks and blues, and a vibrant, verdant green.

He tipped his head down, needing to see Blaze. The colors pulsed then vanished, leaving his vision clear.

A song unlike any he'd heard filled the air, pulsing like a heartbeat between them. Blaze's eyes were still open, still focused on him. Orange and red streaked through the irises as Blaze arched his back, wet heat spreading behind Griff as Blaze came again.

The song grew, and the rhythm doubled. Griff shook, and the feelings inside him overwhelmed him. He struggled to breathe, his head spun and darkness encased him a moment later.

Chapter Nine

"Can you *not* act with honor at *all?*" King Fyre shouted, two hot jets of steam powering from his nostrils and just missing Blaze's head. "All you had to do was help King Artaxis, and instead you end up… Argh!" King Fyre smacked himself on the forehead.

Queen Bonny tutted and turned a glittering orange stare on Blaze. "Really, Blaze. A *fairy?* Are you that desperate for affection?"

Anger welled within Blaze and bubbled over the bands of his restraint. "What do you mean, *a fairy?* And what's it to you if I *am* desperate for affection? Who doesn't need to be touched?"

Bonny narrowed her eyes and stood, rising from her throne like a goddess come to life. "That does not mean you can go around fucking fairies."

"Why not?" Blaze asked, glaring back at her. "Why do you get to decide where my dick goes?"

"Blaze!" King Fyre snapped. "That's uncalled for!"

"*Her* judging me for wanting to be wanted is what's uncalled for!" Blaze shouted, gesturing at Bonny. "And why should she have any say anyway? She's not my mother!"

"No, but I *am* your queen, something you seem to have forgotten." Bonny pointed one lean talon-tipped finger at him. The electric shock that hit Blaze knocked him on his ass. "You will not take such a tone with me."

Pain enveloped him, and Blaze toppled onto his back as he gasped.

"You will always show me respect," Queen Bonny said. "Even when we are in a more relaxed environment. But especially when we are in the Throne Room and you are awaiting judgment!"

Blaze flopped like a fish out of water as she continued tormenting him.

"Honey, I think that's, er, uncalled for," King Fyre said tentatively. "He is my little brother, after all."

Bonny sighed and lowered her hand. "I wasn't going to toast him. He'll be fine. Consider it a paddling for an adult."

The agony ceased in an instant, but Blaze was stunned and not ready to move. Instead, he kept his eyes closed and ignored the king and queen as they bickered or whatever they were doing.

Yes, yes, he'd crossed a line he shouldn't have. He'd had intimate relations with another species, which was definitely frowned upon, but mainly because of the offspring that could result. That wasn't a problem for two males.

Well that, and of course dragons tended to think they were better than all the other species.

A longing that hurt almost as much as Bonny's punishment stirred in Blaze's chest. He clutched at his heart, curling into a ball. The song that had filled the air when Griff had climaxed wrapped around him and infiltrated his thoughts.

There was Griff, so beautiful, perfect, powerful. That song, the colors that had enveloped Blaze and the fairy, like the air itself was turned into a rainbow around them—nothing like that had ever happened to Blaze before.

Griff had sighed and lain down on him. Blaze had a few moments of perfection in his life, holding Griff, listening to his breaths, feeling the smooth, warm skin against his.

Then all hells had broken loose. And now he was in more trouble than ever, and he couldn't—wouldn't—regret what he and Griff had done together.

* * * *

One moment, Griff had been sleeping better than he had in a long time. He'd felt some strong internal tug, some spiritual pull at his core when he'd climaxed. But he'd kept back the last of the binding words.

He'd still felt so close to Blaze, so safe, that he'd let sleep take him. Only to wake up to frantic pounding on the door and Gia on the other side, screeching to the high heavens that Blaze had kidnapped Griff.

That was all it had taken. The door had been magicked away, Griff had been yanked off Blaze, and asinine accusations had flown. Blaze had been carted off by fairies, and Griff didn't know where he'd been taken to. Away from the castle the fairies were in, he would guess.

His gut cramped, and Griff curled over onto his side.

"Oh, stop pouting," Gia said. "I didn't know you two had done the deed. I thought he'd abducted you or something. You don't have sex with random strangers anymore. What was I supposed to think?"

"Maybe that I can act as I choose in regards to things such as sex?" Griff snapped, holding himself tightly. Gods, but he ached all the way to his bones. His head pounded, and that was not a pleasant experience at all. "I wouldn't go busting in on you."

"But…" Gia sighed. "A *dragon*, Griff? Really? When King Artaxis has let it be known more than once that he wants you in his harem?"

It wasn't an unusual thing in a Love fairy's life, to be in a harem with relatives. Sex was…freer for their kind. Even so, Griff had never been able to stomach the idea of it.

And his king didn't appeal to him in a sexual way. None of the fairies in his frolic interested him. Griff knew he was lucky in that Artaxis didn't force him into the harem—kings could do whatever they wanted with their subjects, after all—but their kind were lovers, not fighters.

And why did he hurt worse with every moment that passed?

"What's wrong with you?" Gia asked, her voice soft with concern.

"There's nothing wrong with what I did with Blaze!" Griff forced himself to uncurl and flop onto his back. He looked at Gia. "Why is it a problem that he's a dragon? He was a man when I was making love with him."

Gia's eyebrows shot up to her hairline. "Making love?"

Griff blushed furiously, the heat of it causing sweat to break out on his upper lip. "Sex. I mean, when I was having sex with him." The cramping in his gut increased. "Oh—" Griff moaned and closed his eyes.

"Griff?" Gia touched his cheek. "You're hot. What's—"

"Why did you take me away from him?" Griff panted out. "You should have left us alone!"

"Oh no. Oh, no no." Gia kept muttering as she ran her hands over him, the cooling power of her healing ability not really helping Griff much. "Griff, what did you do? *What did you do?*"

Chapter Ten

"Blaze! *Blaze!*"

Blaze groaned, his head pounding much like it wanted to just explode. At least that would end his misery.

"Blaze, brother, open your eyes." The urgency in the voice pulled at Blaze.

He wasn't sure when the last time someone had sounded so worried about him, so that was a shocker. *Oh. Shock. Shocked. Shit!*

Blaze whimpered when his shoulder was gripped and given a hard shake.

"Blaze!"

"Ow," he whined, trying to get his hands to move, needing to cradle his noggin and cushion it against the gods-awful nag ripping him from sleep.

But he remembered the shock, and Bonny, and Griff—Blaze forced his eyelids open. It took as much effort as anything in his life ever had. Maybe more.

His vision was blurry.

"Blaze?"

Wait, he knew that voice. Blaze tried to speak, but his mouth and throat were dry and he instead made an embarrassing bleating noise.

"Shit! She fried your brain, didn't she?" King Fyre muttered. "What am I going to —"

"Nngh." Well, that wasn't a word. Even Blaze could tell in his screwed-up state. He blinked and swallowed a few times, then was able to make out his brother's face. Sheesh, Fyre looked like he'd spent a night in the lowest level of all hells. "Whaa?"

Fyre wasn't wearing his kingly gear. The ridiculous jewel-encrusted crown and heavy gold and purple robes were gone. A wave of yearning hit Blaze. *This* was his brother Fyre, not the king, and Blaze didn't get to see him often anymore.

Fyre eased Blaze into a sitting position, guiding him with a gentle but firm grip. "Gods, I'm sorry. I didn't know she'd do that."

Blaze found himself propped against a pile of pillows, seated atop an ornate bed that was not his. The gilt and gold and decorative overkill clued him in. "Why'm I in your room?"

Fyre pushed some hair off Blaze's brow, then tucked some more behind his left ear. Tears stung Blaze's eyes. He closed them and tucked his chin to his chest. "What?" He didn't even know what he meant by that one word — it just slipped out.

Fyre's heavy sigh gusted across his cheek. "I love Bonny, but sometimes she scares me. I don't always think she does the right thing, but she doesn't always do the wrong thing, either. This time…" Another wistful exhalation. "This time, she overstepped. I'm sorry, little brother."

"You always think I'm a pest," Blaze muttered, unable to keep the accusation back. "You think I'm a total fuckup."

Fyre cupped his chin. "Look at me."

Blaze didn't want to. He liked hiding behind his eyelids. But he knew Fyre. He'd wait until Blaze obeyed, even if it took all night. So Blaze opened one eye, a little.

Fyre snorted, amusement making him grin. "You are stubborn and unique, and I love everything about you, even the troublemaking part."

Well, Blaze had known that he was a pain in the ass.

"Stop it," Fyre snapped. "Whatever you're thinking, just stop it. You aren't—what'd you say I thought you were? A pest and a total fuckup?"

Blaze nodded, gulping down a knot of emotion that threatened to choke him. "Yeah."

"I have never said anything like that," Fyre growled. "I've never put you down, and not once have I regretted raising you! Stop putting your own insecurities on me. Projecting, right? You think those things, and just assume everyone else does, but we don't. *I* don't."

Blaze really hoped that wasn't a tear slipping out the corner of his eye. "But I can't—"

"No, don't start that. You start with what you *can* do." Fyre let go of his chin and sat back on his butt. "Apparently, that includes seducing fairies. At least your fairy wasn't part of King Artaxis's harem after all. That would have been a nightmare."

"He's not?" Blaze suddenly felt a lot better than he had. His heart even seemed to tingle and beat faster. "Griff's not a part of the harem?" he asked just for extra clarification.

Fyre shook his head. "No. However —"

Blaze cringed. "However's never good."

"You're telling me," Fyre groused, glaring at the ceiling. "Artaxis was not happy about you and this… Griff-fairy getting it on. He's very protective of Griff."

"How unhappy?" Blaze sat up straighter, the need to go find Griff hitting him much like Bonny's bolt had. "Is Griff in trouble? I'll tell Artaxis it was all me. I'll tell him Griff felt sorry for me and —"

"He isn't in trouble, and you will do no such thing." Fyre got up and paced a few steps. "Artaxis said Griff is vulnerable because his brain has been damaged, and he has no wings."

Blaze frowned and pictured Griff. He hadn't even noticed the lack of wings, though if he had, he'd likely just have believed the fairies could make them go away. Was that possible? "He's supposed to have wings?"

Fyre turned back toward him. "Yes. All the fairies flew in, remember? Except Griff." He arched one brow at Blaze. "According to this Griff's sister, you should know how Griff arrived."

Blaze blushed hot from head to toes. He wanted to look away from Fyre but didn't. "On a dragonfly. I screwed up." Pain shot through Blaze, and he wasn't sure if it was physical or not. "I could have killed him because I wasn't paying attention." Gods, his chest burned, and something deep inside him felt like it was going to break.

Fyre knelt on the bed, his expression once more conveying concern. "Blaze? What's wrong?"

Blaze pressed both hands to his chest. "I can't think of what could have happened. It makes me ache."

Fyre touched Blaze's top hand. "Just breathe."

Blaze tried, but he couldn't stop fretting about Griff. "His brain is hurt? How? Where are his wings, if he's supposed to have them? Why am I in trouble for having sex with him? He came to me. He..." Blaze shivered with the memory of what he was about to say. "He took control. He wasn't hesitant. If his brain *is* hurt, I saw no evidence of it."

Fyre hummed and patted Blaze's hand. "Is that so? He came to you, and he, er, took control? I'm still not thrilled about the interspecies thing, but...but you seem to really like the fairy, and you two won't make some odd fairy-dragon hybrid. Am I right in what I'm thinking that you like this guy? That you want more than just this one sexual experience with him?"

Blaze cleared his throat. "Yeah?"

Fyre snickered and gave him a nudge. "Scoot over. I need some room, then I'm going to call a snack for us and some wine, and I'll tell you all that I know about your Griff."

Blaze scrambled over to allow his brother to share the bed with him. This camaraderie was so strange and so much like what Blaze craved from his brother. He was probably still unconscious, dreaming this all.

"Why was I in so much trouble before?"

"Because we overreacted," Fyre admitted, and it sounded like he might have actually been pained by having to say so. "I thought you'd banged someone from the harem, and there'd be a war with the fairies. We could defeat them easily, but..." He shrugged. "And being the king, sometimes I...I screw up, brother. I should have listened. When you didn't wake up right away, and you started moaning and —" Fyre inhaled shakily. "I thought —"

Blaze didn't want to hear any more of that. "I'm not dead," he pointed out. But he still hurt, that deep, in-the-core pain that was steady, not fading. He had a craving that wasn't related to food or drink. He lusted for Griff, and it was all he could do to keep himself there, on the bed, with his brother. Even though he appreciated the time and attention, and he desired the closeness with Fyre, he felt the need to be somewhere else.

He wanted Griff, to see him and hear him, make sure he was okay. "Griff's not in trouble?" he asked again, clenching his hands against the blanket.

"No, I don't think so. Artaxis is furious with you, as is that Gia-fairy, but they said nothing of Griff being in trouble." Fyre scowled. "And I'd hope that this attraction you feel for your fairy works both ways, and he doesn't play himself off as the victim."

Blaze didn't believe himself to be the smartest dragon around, but even he figured that one out. "He won't, or else Artaxis would be back here, demanding my head."

"True enough," Fyre agreed. He sighed as he got comfortable, then pressed the button by the headboard that would have a servant racing up to the room. "So, we've established that you and Griff were consensual lovers, that Bonny and I overreacted. You like Griff. I don't see the attraction, but hey, whatever sparks your fire. Now, about his injuries…"

Blaze tensed up at the plural usage there, but he kept his mouth shut, and he listened as his brother talked.

Chapter Eleven

"You did *what?*" Gia shrieked. "Are you stupid?"

Griff threw his purple shoes at her, both with one decent toss. "I'm neither stupid nor deaf," he said calmly, though inside he felt like a troll turd. At least the agonizing pain had stopped and it was now only a dull throb.

"But you were saying the binding words!" Gia continued, dodging both shoes easily. "Griff, come on, I'm not trying to be a twatwaddle, but you're telling me you might be mated to the dragon shifter! You don't even know him! How could you let your control slip like that?"

"I wish I knew more bad words," Griff muttered, sitting on the bed. "You should have some bad words tossed your way for all the shouting you keep doing. Gia, my head *hurts*. Stop already."

Gia huffed and puffed and finally sat on the floor in front of him. She looked at him with compassion and concern, and Griff wanted to cry.

"I'm worried about you," Gia said quietly.

That was the last straw. Griff's defenses collapsed just like he did. He flopped backward and shoved a pillow over his face as he stopped trying to hold back the tears.

"Oh, sweetheart," Gia said, sliding onto the bed to lie beside him. "Come here. I'm sorry I was so harsh. I'm just scared, and we have no one but Artaxis to ask about this."

"No," Griff managed to say, lifting an edge of the pillow. "I call a sibling swear. You can't tell him."

"Argh." Gia pushed a tissue under the pillow. "Here. Don't get snot all over the pillow. You have to rest your head on it tonight."

Despite his foul mood and achy everything, and despite the fact that he might have done something more stupid than Gia had accused him of being, Griff laughed.

"That sibling swear is outdated," Gia mumbled. "We're grown-ups now."

"But still siblings, so it stands," Griff pointed out. He gave his sister a wobbly smirk. "You are bound by it."

"I know," she groaned. "The hardships of being your favorite sister."

"My *only* sister," Griff said, the argument a familiar one he could remember even despite his injury.

"That you know of," Gia shot back at him right on time. "Mom wasn't monogamous at all. She didn't stick to our kind of fairies, either. That's why she said our fathers could be anyone in the fairy kingdoms, just about. Who knows where she went off to."

Griff often wondered. "She left when we were just kids, right? I'm not remembering *that* wrong?"

"Yes, not even in double digits yet." Gia shrugged like it didn't matter, but Griff knew it hurt. "Guess she had better things to do."

"Maybe something happened to her, like it did to me," Griff said without thinking. He put the pillow aside. "I'm sorry. Don't be upset."

Gia sniffed. "I'm not. You could be right. I suppose it makes me a rotten fairy to hope that there's a reason she abandoned us other than she just didn't love us enough to hang around."

Well, when she put it like that, Griff was wounded that their mom had vanished, too.

"I didn't have to try to remember the way to his room," Griff said a moment later, sharing with his sister even though he suspected he might regret it.

Gia sat up and stared at him.

Griff fidgeted with the blankets. "What?"

"You remembered where his room was?"

Griff couldn't tell if she was surprised or irritated. "No. I traced it out on my window, but I didn't have to look at it. I just found him, on my own."

"No wrong turns?" she asked, tipping her chin down at him.

"None, and before you ask, I'm sure." Griff closed his eyes and imagined it. "The path to his room was the clearest one I've ever taken."

"Oh, hells and demon spawn," Gia groaned. "You *are* his mate."

Griff's heart stuttered. "But a fairy and a dragon?"

Gia poked him in the belly. "Why not?"

"Because it hasn't happened before!" Griff exclaimed.

Gia pulled one of his eyelids open. "Someone's gotta go first, so why not you and dragon boy? Hey, is he hung like a dragon?"

"Gia!" Griff whipped his head aside and opened both eyes before she ended up damaging him somehow. "Gah!"

"Prude," she teased. "I mean, he *is* a dragon shifter." Then she became serious. "I don't know how Artaxis is going to handle having one of his fairies mated to a dragon shifter."

As bad as Griff wanted to say it was none of Artaxis's business, it kind of was. That was the way things were in the magical realm. In each species, the king or queen ruled, period.

But Griff had a rather brilliant idea, and it perked him right up. "Artaxis wanted an alliance with the dragons…"

Gia's lips parted. "Ohhhh, I like the way you think."

It might not have been the alliance Artaxis wanted, but if Blaze held any authority at all, had any important connections, then it might be beneficial for the Love fairies in the long run if Griff was mated to Blaze.

He still thought *if*, because he hadn't said that last line, so he wasn't convinced he was fully attached to Blaze.

Never mind the dull ache, the longing, the worry or that horrible, horrible pain he'd felt earlier. "Gia, would I know if Blaze was hurting? I mean, if the mate bond happened, would I feel what he felt?"

Gia frowned. "I have no idea. Maybe? It depends on the connection. You didn't say the last line, but I think…" She took a deep breath, then expelled it. "Maybe you didn't have to. Maybe the connection between you and, er, Blaze, was so strong you didn't have to say it. You just had to, you know, think it."

Griff gawked at her, speechless as he did so. He really did need to learn more bad words.

Chapter Twelve

Blaze didn't have to worry about sneaking out of the main castle silently. With all the shouting coming from Fyre and Bonny's quarters, and *alllllllllll* the eager eavesdroppers — although, was it eavesdropping when they were yelling so loudly no one could avoid hearing them? — were lurking closer so they could watch the doors and see if Bonny or Fyre ran out. Or were thrown out. Either was possible, what with the ruckus they were making.

So it was no hardship for Blaze to slip out of the castle, where he had been told to stay, and into the night. Fyre had said it was for his own safety since the fairy king might want to hurt Blaze for what he and Griff had done.

Blaze was willing to take that risk. He needed to see Griff and make sure he was okay. Knowing now that the adorable fairy had been injured in what should have been an impossible manner, Blaze felt the need to comfort him, and reassure himself that Griff was still there.

But Fyre had said Griff's memory was screwed up. What if Griff didn't remember him?

The pain in his chest was entirely out of order, Blaze decided, even as he rubbed at it. He shouldn't be so attached to Griff.

And yet, there he was, tiptoeing past the guards at the palace gates. Both guards were snoring. Blaze might have to mention that to Fyre if he could find a way to do it without landing himself in a steaming heap of trouble.

Blaze noted the moon, a bare sliver of light that seemed to flicker. An enchanted moon, that was what it was called, when something in the atmosphere caused such an effect.

It always freaked Blaze the hells out. He was afraid one night he'd look up, see the moon waver, then it'd explode and they'd all die.

Sometimes, just *sometimes*, he was given to melodrama and paranoia. At least he had enough sense not to tell anyone else.

The castle the fairies were in was lit up, every window shining with a bright light. Blaze stopped behind a row of golden hedges and tried to figure out his next move. Sneaking in to find Griff wasn't going to be possible if everyone in the stupid place was still awake.

And fucking. They were probably all fucking, except hopefully not Griff.

Blaze scampered over to the next row of hedges. From there, he could see Griff's window. He stared as hard as possible—which, surprisingly, made his eyes throb.

"Come on, Griff. Come to the window. Let me see you." Blaze whispered the words, clenching his hands into fists as he forced himself to stay behind the hedges. The driving need to see Griff was making him twitch.

Blaze considered the possibility that he'd lost his damned mind.

"Griff, what did you do to me?" *Okay, not fair to put all the blame on the fairy.* Blaze had been a very, *very* active participant.

And Griff had been the most skilled, exquisite lover in Blaze's life.

Not that he had a huge backlist of lovers.

Blaze leaned forward and got smacked in the face with what he thought was a random branch. He cursed and tumbled onto his butt.

A buzz sounded in his ears.

Blaze blinked. No. A buzz sounded in *one* ear. *By* one ear, to be precise. He turned his head and got head-butted between the eyes by an angry dragonfly.

"Stop," he hissed when the thing came after him again. Blaze ended up flat on his back, digging his fingers into the dirt lest he do something dumb like swat at the dragonfly. He was almost one-hundred-percent positive that it was the same one Griff had flown in on. Either that, or it was just a vicious, psychotic dragonfly that was attacking him. There were probably breeds of them like that.

"I'm sorry," Blaze bit out, turning his head to avoid another thump. It wasn't particularly painful. In fact, the slight tap didn't hurt at all. But it was frustrating, and his eyes crossed every time the dragonfly dive-bombed him, because Blaze tried to watch the critter.

"I said I'm sorry!" Blaze exclaimed a little louder than he'd meant to speak. "Stop it! I'm sorry! If you think I'm that much of an ass, you'd be stupid to keep attacking me, don't you think?"

The dragonfly shot backward, and Blaze could have been wrong, but he thought the rapid buzzing sound was probably the insect's way of cussing him out.

Blaze looked up at the moon. "Any time now," he muttered to it. "Just put me out of my misery. I'm being held prisoner by a dragonfly. This is what my life's become."

The mini-whine got him another round of buzzing and dodging. Blaze really needed to stop getting himself into these kinds of messes.

He got to his knees, then to his feet. Why was he cowering? He was a lot bigger than the dragonfly. And he could run.

Blaze got precisely one step in before the dragonfly zipped in front of him and hovered at eye level with him. "What do you want from me?"

The thing buzzed and buzzed, and seemed to be doing some kind of insane insect dance.

"I—" Blaze snapped his mouth shut when the dragonfly dove at him. He scampered backward. Gods, he was being herded by an insect the size of his pinky finger!

When the dragonfly flew past him, Blaze turned his head to follow its flight—and gasped, his heart doing an odd *thump-flop-thump*.

Griff seemed equally shocked to see him. "Blaze? You're here?"

Was it possible the dragonfly had been trying to help him all along?

Blaze didn't care. "Yeah," he croaked, taking in the vision Griff made, with his long white hair loose and flowing to his waist. He looked ethereal, though Blaze knew him to be strong. "How—?"

Griff's pale skin glowed in the scant moonlight. His eyes sparkled as if glitter had been spilled into the irises. He approached Blaze slowly, as if he were afraid to spook him off, perhaps.

"I can't believe you're really here. I thought…" Griff shook his head.

Blaze didn't know what to say. Every word he might have spoken turned to ash when Griff stopped an inch from him.

"I want to kiss you," Griff said.

The answer must have shown on Blaze's face. An instant later, he closed his arms around Griff and moaned as he tasted the sweet man's lips.

Chapter Thirteen

There was no use pretending Gia hadn't been right. Griff knew it the moment he'd felt compelled to come outside. He just hadn't expected Blaze to be so close.

And to see him, his vibrant hair and freckles muted by the dim moonlight, but his face still as pale as the moon itself — Griff's breath had been stolen by the man's very presence.

Then his heart was stolen as well by the way Blaze just melted for him, the sweet taste of his lips and the press of that big, warm body to his. Blaze met him like an eager puppy, warm and wiggly, wanting to be touched and loved on.

Griff never stood a chance.

The moment Blaze's arms went around him, Griff moaned and latched on to his mate. Blaze canted his head, and their mouths sealed together even better.

Griff had never experienced such intense arousal. It was both freeing and frightening.

Blaze slid his big hands down to Griff's backside and squeezed. The frightening part of it vanished. Pure heat wrapped with lust took its place, and Griff climbed Blaze like a mountain, getting his legs wrapped around the man's slim waist so he could rub to their hearts' content.

Although it wasn't their hearts that were getting rubbed.

And there wasn't enough friction to satisfy either one of them, but it felt so good to just rut and rut, until Griff just had to have more.

Blaze kept dipping his hands down, cupping, kneading, pushing his fingers into Griff's crease.

Griff wanted his clothes off. He wanted Blaze's clothes off. He wanted more sex and less sexual frustration.

He lowered his legs down, then kept going, leaving those succulent lips for more southern territory.

"Griff," Blaze rasped, "I—"

Griff didn't like the expression on Blaze's face, like he was close to regretting this already. Griff plucked at Blaze's nipples through his thin shirt and that took care of Blaze trying to speak.

At least until Griff bit one of those taut little nipples.

"Griff!" Blaze trembled like he was breaking from the inside out.

Griff chuckled, so pleased with the way Blaze reacted to him.

Then Blaze tweaked one of Griff's nipples, and he barely kept from coming. That red-hot reaction worked both ways.

Griff shed his clothing, shrugging out of the half-tunic easily. "Now you," he said, eager to see and touch all of Blaze's bare skin.

Blaze went for his waistband, and Griff went after his shirt. They had Blaze nude almost as fast as Griff had stripped.

"Gods, you're perfect," Griff whispered, watching a bead of sweat roll slowly down Blaze's chest.

"No, you are," Blaze said. He reached for and palmed Griff's cock. "Can I suck it?"

Griff gripped Blaze's shoulders and tugged. "Yes. No, wait."

Blaze frowned. "Wait? I—you don't want—?"

"Oh, but I *do*."

Griff was a fairy, a creature of nature. It wasn't strange to him at all to guide Blaze onto the thick grass a few feet away, to stretch out beside him and let the dew cool their heated skin.

Griff kissed Blaze again. The things he wanted to do to the dragon shifter...

He nibbled on Blaze's lips, down his jaw and neck, leaving purple marks behind. He laved Blaze's nipples and worked them to stiff peaks, pinching, biting, until the skin on both was hot and a deeper shade of coral.

Then he moved down, his own cock heavy with need, his balls drawing up. If he didn't hurry, he'd come before he got to feel Blaze's mouth on his shaft. Gods, but Griff did love blow jobs.

He pushed more needy sounds from Blaze when he lapped at Blaze's belly button. Blaze's thick cock was leaving sticky strings of pre-cum on his belly, and Griff moved to lap those up.

Then he moved around until he had his cock close to Blaze's face. "Now you can suck it."

"Thank the gods," Blaze grumped. "I thought I was—*oomph!*"

Yes, Griff knew just how to stop the griping. He pressed the tip of his cock in deeper and shuddered. Gods, it felt so good. Blaze's mouth was wet and hot and perfect with the suction, that tongue of his flicking all over.

"Blaze," Griff rasped, eyes rolling. He had to get some control over himself or he was going to come in an embarrassingly short period of time.

Griff pulled Blaze's cock right to his mouth and started licking the crown. The smoky flavor was addictive, and Griff needed more. He closed his eyes and sucked, taking Blaze's length in while Blaze did the same for him.

Griff fondled Blaze's balls and moaned around Blaze's cock when Blaze palmed Griff's nuts. Blaze soon mirrored his actions perfectly, and Griff lost himself in the pleasure his lover was sharing with him.

He sucked and touched, licked and caressed. Griff neither knew nor cared how long he and Blaze sucked each other. The blissful minutes sped by, and the arousal inside him grew more and more urgent.

That music started up in Griff's head again, and goosebumps pebbled his skin. He thrust into Blaze's mouth, then pulled back and did it again.

Griff worked Blaze's shaft, using more suction and pressing up on those tight, tight balls.

Blaze thrust jerkily into his mouth, once, twice, then his cock swelled and he arched, releasing Griff's dick and keening as cum spurted into Griff's mouth.

Griff swallowed and swallowed. It seemed like Blaze came even more than the first time. That music didn't cease, either, and Griff was unable to stop himself from thinking the words, mouthing them around Blaze's cock.

Then Blaze jolted, his shaft slipping from Griff's mouth. From one heartbeat to the next, Griff was turned over onto his back, with Blaze going after Griff's dick like it was the last one Blaze would ever see.

Blaze sucked him hungrily, masterfully, pressing down on Griff's thighs as he bobbed his head.

And Griff felt it, the way Blaze was moving his lips, flicking his tongue in perfect synchronicity to the song that would — and likely already had — bound them to one another.

Griff arched, a lightning bolt of ecstasy shooting through him. He gasped and panted, losing himself completely as his climax began.

The words weren't just in his head this time. They escaped from his lips when he meant to shout and fled into the air to strengthen the invisible bond between them.

This time, Griff didn't fight it. This time, he knew it wasn't just him experiencing it. This time, Blaze was there with him, in his head, and that knowledge catapulted Griff into an orgasm that felt it would leave him turned inside out from the pleasure.

His fingers and toes tingled first, then a rapturous sensation spread out from Griff's balls to his cock, then to all points in his body.

He shook and thrust, bucked and ground his teeth until he had to unclench them, had to breathe and the release began to ebb.

Eventually, he was able to open his eyes and blink blearily at the sky.

"That kinda sex is going to kill us," Blaze said from beside him.

Griff chuckled and moved to lie beside Blaze. He turned his head and found Blaze staring right at him.

Blaze gulped, then got a determined look in his eyes. "What just happened between us?"

Then it was Griff's turn to gulp. *Gods, I'm a coward!* No, he wasn't, he *wasn't*. "I, er, we…we bonded."

Blaze sat up so fast his movement was a blur. "Bonded? As in, mates?" he asked in a strained voice.

Griff realized that Blaze might not be thrilled to be bonded to a fairy, especially not a brain-damaged, wingless one.

But he was bonded to him nonetheless. "Yes."

Blaze gawked at him, then surprised him by collapsing into a heap of laughing — no, guffawing — man.

"What?" Griff asked him. "What's so funny?"

It took Blaze a minute to calm down enough to answer. "Oh, man. This is going to really piss off the queen! I bet your king isn't happy about it, either." Then he beamed at Griff. "It's a good thing I've always had issues with authority."

Chapter Fourteen

Blaze's continued amusement confused Griff. "I still don't understand why you're laughing." Why wasn't he mad at being bonded to a messed-up fairy? And how could he find it entertaining to anger the queen? Griff wasn't looking forward to telling Artaxis about what had happened, and he sure didn't think it was funny.

"Blaze?"

Blaze swiped at his eyes and chuckled for another minute or so, shaking his head. "Ah, man. I can't help it. Sorry." Then he surprised Griff by pulling him into a gentle hug. "Don't look so scared, Griff. We'll be okay."

Had he looked scared? Griff examined his emotions. Well, probably, considering he *was* scared. "But why would you laugh? Why aren't you running away from me? Why —"

Blaze cupped his chin. "Hey."

Griff's heart thudded heavily as he raised his eyes to Blaze's. The tenderness he saw in those fiery depths warmed him through and through.

"Don't panic, okay?" Blaze asked. "I know I'm not the greatest prize—a dragon who can't control his fire. No one's ever wanted me enough to bond with me. I've burned people, dragons, on accident before. But when I'm with you, I feel..." He trailed off, eyes almost closing.

Griff licked his dry lips. "You feel what?"

Blaze pulled him closer. "Mmm. Yeah, I feel like I'm not rattling apart inside. Calm, even when I'm so flustered with need. Like you center me, or act as a...a touchstone, a talisman, a— Oh crap." He exhaled, rolling his eyes. "I don't have the words, okay? But I feel you here." Blaze placed Griff's right hand over his heart. "And it's no surprise to me when I think about that, and the fact that we bonded. Dragons hardly ever do, you know."

Griff was reeling from the touching confession. And the touching, period. But he was surprised by that bit of information. "Really? Hardly ever? Why not?"

Blaze shrugged and urged Griff's hand a little lower, nudging it down from his chest toward his belly. "Dunno. We just don't. Mostly dragons fuck and fight and pair up when those two things work well together. I think, according to rumors, the last time a dragon shifter bonded was a few hundred years ago." His eyes widened. "Ha! And if that's right, not just talk, she bonded to a mermaid!"

"Fire and water," Griff mused, somewhat distracted by all the muscled belly under his palm.

"Yeah, fire and water. We're fire and, um..." Blaze clenched those wonderful abs.

"Fairies have no elemental power," Griff explained, running his fingers over the deep groove bisecting Blaze's stomach. "We're just magic." Sadness threatened to dim his enjoyment of this time spent with Blaze, and Griff buried it away for now. "Except I'm not, because I have no wings, and my memory is a mess."

"You're still magic," Blaze said quietly. "More magic, even, because you're still here."

"Where else would I be?" Griff asked, canting his head so he could see Blaze's expression.

Blaze gulped and shook his head. "You could have not survived, and we'd never have met."

Sometimes Griff had thought dying would have been for the best, but he tried to avoid those dark, self-pitying moments. "Will your queen really be angry?"

Blaze snorted, smoke puffs shooting from his nostrils. "Oh yeah. She put the hurt on me earlier for — ah, anyway. Yeah, she won't be pleased. My brother — he's the king—he'll be worried about pissing her off, and your king. Well, probably more about pissing off Bonny. He has to live with her."

Griff's stomach cramped. "Bonny's the queen?" He thought of a smiling, sweet lady with a name like that, not the cruel shrew it was sounding like she was.

"Yeah, short for Bonfire. She's got a hot temper, even for a dragon," Blaze explained. "Comes from being born in the lava pits in Planzatillo."

Planzatillo was on the other side of the world, where little survived but dragons, the Fire fairies and demons. It was rumored to be a very brutal area, though Griff knew of no one who'd ever been there...and come back. That he could remember.

"She hurt you?" His belly cramping was growing more intense. Hadn't he hurt, badly, earlier? Or was he misremembering?

Blaze tried to pull away. Griff wrapped his arms around the gorgeous dragon. "Blaze? She did, didn't she? Because of me?" Guilt tightened like a vise around Griff's chest. "She hurt you."

When Blaze still didn't answer, Griff's guilt merged with anger. "She hurt you, because you were with me — a fairy? Because of what I am? Because she was afraid of my king's reaction? My king won't be pleased, but he'd never hurt me! Not now, especially, when he learns you're my bonded. He won't like it, because Love fairies hardly ever..." Griff blinked. "Bond."

"Weird," Blaze mumbled. "Two species that don't really bond, and here we are...bonded."

"And your queen will hurt you again." Griff wanted to hit her, though Love fairies shouldn't ever be prone to such behavior. They were all about love, unless provoked. They'd defend their own, and their allies, to the death. "She hurt you, and it burned inside you."

Blaze frowned. "How do you know that?"

Griff shivered. "I felt it," he admitted huskily. "Like an angry burst of fire, inside me."

"Gods be damned, that witch," Blaze snarled, tensing up until he felt as if he were made of stone. "Hurting me is one thing. I can deal with it. But hurting you? Not acceptable. Not even retroactively. Wait. Is that the right word?" He huffed. "Fuck! I mean, she hurt you already, and no, I won't let that pass. No one hurts you again, not you. I'll—" He growled, hands fisting.

Griff was afraid of what Blaze would do. There was a definite promise of violence in his voice. "Blaze? You can't be mad at her for hurting me when she didn't know that's what she was doing." But Griff could sure not like her for hurting Blaze. "Does she always resort to violence?"

"Seems to be her way."

Griff wasn't sure about the wisdom of his next question but didn't know how else to get through to Blaze. Heck, he didn't even know Blaze! "And you want to be like her? To use violence before considering any other options?"

"Oh, damn it all," Blaze groused, but the edges of his lips curled up in a grin. "You just undid my temper with that first question, you know? Because no, I don't want to be like her." Then he shuddered. "And *ew*. She screws my brother, so that's really, *really* gross. No way do I wanna be like her!"

Griff giggled. He was relieved to have helped Blaze out, but there was still the very real threat to him from that queen.

And, admittedly, Artaxis wouldn't be thrilled. It'd be within his power to even break the bond if he wanted to, especially since it was a newly established bond. At least, that was the way Griff thought it was. Gods, he wished he could remember for sure.

"Why are you frowning?" Blaze asked. "You should only be happy, but not that creepy kind of happy where you walk around all day and night with a big, toothy smile and crazy eyes. Not that you would, but I was thinking about this guy who was actually a gryphon shifter and he had an addiction to this plant that is usually toxic to most— Well anyway, he always smiled, and it wasn't anything like your smile so maybe never mind all of this and just—"

Griff kissed him, hard, deep and sincerely. How could he not fall for a man who could ramble on like that? And as they kissed, a crazy, wild idea began to form in Griff's mind.

Chapter Fifteen

When Griff kissed him like that, Blaze could hardly keep from rolling onto his belly and begging Griff to fuck him. Blaze held back, however. He was a little nervous about getting fucked.

And what they were doing felt so good, the way Griff moaned softly when they rutted against each other.

Yeah, it was beyond good. Blaze cupped Griff's butt. He was certain they'd both get off in a matter of minutes just from humping on each other.

But Griff pulled back, panting.

Blaze blinked and loosened his grip on the fairy. "Wha's wrong?" Oh wow. His tongue felt thick and heavy, his lips hot and swollen from those kisses.

Griff shook his head, pressing a hand to his chest.

Blaze put his hand over Griff's. "You okay?" Concern had him focused. "Something wrong?"

Griff giggled, albeit breathlessly, then winked at him before standing up. "You just arouse me to the point where I feel like I'll combust if I don't have you."

"Well, we can't have you combusting," Blaze purred, rising as well and moving closer to Griff once again. "So—"

"But I was trying to think," Griff cut in.

Blaze groaned and covered his face with his hands. "Aw, man. Thinking instead of fucking—that's never fun. Can't we just have sex?"

"Just?"

Blaze peeked between his fingers at Griff. "You know what I mean."

Griff's expression was hard to read. "You mean, you want me to fuck you?"

Blaze clenched his ass, his pucker almost aching. "Er, well I thought…"

Griff gestured at him to go on.

"Urm." Why did he get the feeling saying what he'd thought was going to land him in deep shit? Blaze knew he wasn't the brightest star in the sky, but he *did* have a bit of a glow left in him—he wasn't totally stupid. He uncovered his face but didn't answer.

But Griff wasn't stupid, either, although judging by his laughter, he *was* amused. "You thought you'd be fucking me, didn't you? Because I'm smaller and skinnier and weaker. Or because my brain—"

"Don't even go there," Blaze growled, shaking a finger at Griff. "Don't you insult me, or you like that."

Griff blushed delicately and averted his gaze. "It's me. I know my brain is messed up, and I don't know why you wouldn't want the bond between us broken so you can be free to have a normal lover."

Blaze had a temper. There was no doubt about it. Right then, he wanted to shake Griff and hug him at the same time. But he knew he'd never do anything that could possibly harm Griff, so the shaking was out.

But Blaze could scowl and snort with the best of them. "You're saying I'm a shallow prick."

Griff jerked his gaze back to Blaze's. "I did not!"

Blaze crossed his arms over his chest. "Yeah, 'cuz I can't want you since you hurt your head?"

"And I can't fly!" Griff cried out. "I'm damaged—"

"You're going to be damaged if you keep making so much noise!"

Blaze spun around, and Griff gasped.

Blaze recognized Griff's sister Gia immediately and clenched his jaw as he moved to keep her from taking Griff away from him again. "No," he growled, putting on his best menacing air.

Gia flapped a hand at him. "Oh, get over yourself. I'm good with whatever makes my brother happy."

"Oh." Well, that took all the steam out of his sails. "Okay. Good. That's…that's good."

"We're bonded," Griff added. "And, er, we're going to get dressed before this conversation goes any further."

Gia nodded. "Please do, and as to the bonding thing… Well, duh. You said it started the first time you two—" She whistled. "So of course if you did it again, the bond must be established."

Blaze didn't trust her. He kept an eye on Gia as he and Griff quickly put their clothes back on. Gia seemed too accepting after calling him all sorts of names before. And he had admittedly had bad experiences with the females in his life. Granted, Bonny was the only female in his life…

"You have to stop doubting yourself because of what happened to you," Gia said, moving closer to Griff. "Your spirit is still the same, whether you can remember everything or not. I can tell you, you're still the same incredible brother of mine you've always been. Different from me, and most of our frolic, sure, but incredible nonetheless. Even a dragon would know how lucky he is to have you for a mate."

"Hey!" Blaze exclaimed, narrowing his eyes at her. "*Even a dragon?*"

Gia shrugged. "You don't seem overly bright. Griff is really smart—he just has memory issues."

"And no wings," Griff said before adding, "Blaze is smart. Be nice, Gia."

Gia rolled her eyes. "If I have to."

"You do," Griff told her. Then he snapped his fingers. "Oh! I was planning on getting you away from here before your queen can hurt you again! I *knew* there was something I was trying to think of, and I remembered!" He bounced on his toes. "I remembered!" But his exuberance was short-lived. "Now, why can't I remember where I lost my wings?"

Gia looked pained.

Blaze had some questions about that whole deal. "Why hasn't your king sought out the thinning of the veil where that occurred?" was the first one, and he lobbed it at Gia. "If someone could harm Griff from the boring realm, isn't that a problem that should be eliminated?"

"Artaxis sent fairies out to look for the thinning of the veil, but none was found," Gia explained. "We know where Griff was headed when he was hurt. There was nothing on the path he'd have been on."

"Maybe I went off-trail," Griff murmured. "I can't remember." He glanced at Gia. "Am I the kind of fairy who'd have done that?"

Gia pursed her lips. "Well, I'd have said no, but you were planning to run off with Blaze, weren't you?"

Griff's entire face lit up. "I was! But only because his queen hurt him. The pain I felt earlier, she was hurting him, Gia. I can't let her do that again."

"Wow, what a bitch," Gia groused. "Maybe instead of running away, you should dethrone her."

"No, no, we can't do that," Blaze protested. "My brother loves her. Or is enchanted. Or bespelled."

"Or being blackmailed," Gia snarked. "Maybe she has some dirt on him that keeps him under her thumb. I noticed she's rather controlling. Saw it when we first got here. I'm glad our king isn't like that."

"But he won't be happy about me and Griff being bonded," Blaze said.

"He'll get over it. Artaxis isn't unreasonable." Gia bit her lip.

Griff shivered. "He could break our bond. Artaxis doesn't think I'm capable of much since I was hurt."

Gia didn't deny it, and Blaze felt a bright burst of anger on Griff's part. For all that Griff did have memory problems, he was still smart and articulate, and he felt things, emotions, for fuck's sake.

Blaze had never been away from his own kind, but now he had someone who was his and to whom he belonged. Didn't that take precedence over *his own kind*?

"How did I know I'd find you here?"

Gia yelped, and Griff squeaked, but Blaze just sighed and watched as his brother floated gracefully down to the ground. Blaze had never been able to do that, to shift from dragon to man in the air and land easily. He always hit the ground hard, unable to control his descent.

But not Fyre. He could shift and fly silently, which could be a real pain in the ass at times—like now, when Blaze wondered how much his brother had overheard.

Well, running away probably wasn't going to happen now. He'd have liked more time to figure out just how to tell Fyre what had happened, but there was no point in putting it off.

He tucked a very tense Griff closer to his side. "We're bonded. You can't make me leave him."

Fyre's eyebrows winged up his forehead. "Wow. Bonded? For real?" Then to Blaze's shock, he started laughing.

Blaze, Gia and Griff exchanged confused looks while Fyre doubled over, cackling like mad.

"Has he lost his mind?" Griff whispered.

"Who could blame him if he did?" Gia replied. "I met his queen. Sheesh."

"Fyre?" Blaze tentatively reached for his brother's shoulder. "Are you okay?"

Fyre gasped a few times, then managed to stand up straight. He wiped at his cheeks. "Ah, yes, yes. It's just—Bonny's going to shit lava over this."

Blaze was shocked by the vulgarity. Fyre generally kept himself above the use of such sayings.

But it *did* fit.

"Well, Artaxis won't be thrilled, but he won't hurt Griff," Gia snapped. "Or Blaze."

"He could break our bond," Griff murmured. "Can you promise me that he won't?"

"Yeah." Fyre angled his chin at Gia. "Can you? Maybe he's no better than Bonny." Fyre's eyes went wide, and he covered his mouth with both hands. "I can't believe I just said that."

Blaze *thought* that was what he said through two layers of flesh and bones.

Gia sniffed and turned her nose up at him. "Whatever. Artaxis is reasonable. He's all for love, too. Sex is fantastic, but if someone finds they're bonded, that is a blessing no one with any sense would seek to revoke. Artaxis is no fool."

"But Bonny is?" Fyre snarled, his eyes flashing with orange and yellow sparks. "I know she isn't perfect, that she—"

"Whatever." Gia flapped her hand at him.

Fyre sputtered and stuttered, nothing comprehensible leaving his mouth.

Gia smirked at him. "Can't believe I interrupted you? Think you're too important for that?"

Fyre managed to close his mouth.

Blaze cleared his throat. "If you two are done flirting—"

"Flirting!" they both shouted, turning on him.

Blaze only shrank back a little. "Hey, I meant, er, arguing. Yeah, arguing. If you two are done arguing, can we get back to me and Griff?"

Fyre and Gia both harrumphed. Fyre stepped around her to stand in front of Blaze.

"As much as I hate to admit it, it might be best if you and Griff disappeared for a while," he said. "Bonny's become more and more...unreasonable, as of late. I don't know..."

"Are you kicking me out of here?" Blaze rasped, aching inside in a way he'd never experienced before.

Chapter Sixteen

"No, No, that's not what—" King Fyre stopped and grimaced. "Well, kind of, but not like you mean. I'm just encouraging you and Griff to take a lovers' holiday."

Blaze looked so hurt that Griff couldn't stand it. He pressed closer to Blaze and glared at Fyre. "How long?" Granted, Griff had been planning to talk Blaze into running away with him, but that was totally different from Blaze being cast out.

"Yeah, how long?" Gia asked, poking King Fyre in the chest. "That's harsh, sending your own brother away."

"I'm not sending him away!" Fyre protested, raising both his hands in surrender. "I'm not! I'm *suggesting* that he and Griff go on a lovely vacation where they can spend uninterrupted time alone and strengthen their bond while I...deal with the fallout here."

Gia scowled. "You mean that—"

"Gia, enough," Griff warned. He thought King Fyre probably meant well, and it sure sounded like he'd be in a heck of a mess with the queen over this. But why? "Why would there be a problem? You and Artaxis wanted to join forces. What better way than this—a joining, a bonding between the two?"

"And for one of the bonded to be the brother of the king, that'd be kind of like royalty," Gia added.

"Kind of?" Blaze asked. "Hey, me and Fyre had the same parents, I'll have you know, and I'm just as royal as he was. Is." He slumped a bit. "Well, I would be if our royalty worked that way."

"I don't understand." Griff was afraid he'd already forgotten something important that had been said in the conversation. "You're royalty?" he asked Blaze. It made sense, but Griff hadn't even thought—

"No, I'm not," Blaze said.

Gia snorted. "That makes no sense, dragon."

"It's the way of our kind," Fyre said. "Only the firstborn have ever been considered royalty. All other siblings born after are commoners. And before you ask, death of the oldest doesn't change that. If the oldest child dies, all other offspring are, er, eliminated in some manner, and the king and queen begin again."

Griff felt as horrified as Gia looked. "That's awful! How could you do that?"

Fyre shook his head. "I haven't. But it's been a very effective method for keeping the younger siblings from murdering the oldest for the throne. It also gives them impetus for protecting the oldest and seeing to his or her health. As far as I know, there's been less than half a dozen instances of a royal cleansing."

Griff thought he might just be sick. "So if you were to die today…"

Bailey Bradford

King Fyre glanced over his shoulder, back toward his palace. "Well, I *have* suggested you and Blaze both slip away for a while."

"You think your queen would kill you?" Gia asked, sounding outraged.

"I think she wouldn't do such a thing intentionally, but lately she's been..." He didn't finish, and after a minute, Blaze took over.

"She's been meaner than a harpy with her tit caught in an orc trap," Blaze said.

"Ouch." Gia grabbed her boobs with both hands. "Those metal teeth." She shuddered.

Blaze nodded. "And I can't leave my brother here to deal with that."

"You don't have your powers back," Fyre pointed out. "And as Bonny took them from you, only she can return them to you before the set period of time she dictated as punishment."

"Unless she were to die," Blaze muttered. "Not that I'm suggesting such a thing. Or hoping for it." He blushed when everyone looked at him. "What? I mean it. She hasn't always been cruel to me. I think she's angry 'cuz she hasn't ever produced an heir and she's running out of time to spit out a princess or prince."

"Running out of time?" Griff asked, glancing from Blaze to Fyre. "What kind of weird laws do you dragons live under?"

"They aren't weird to us," Fyre retorted. "They've kept our species alive and thriving for many millennia."

"So have ours, and we don't kick out a queen for being infertile," Gia snapped. "Gods, you dragons —"

"No, you fairies have just broken off into a hundred sub-frolics, unable to get along if any of you are the

95

slightest bit different, so you have Love fairies and Water fairies and—" Fyre flapped his hands in the air. "This is a ridiculous argument." He focused his orange gaze on his brother. "Please, just escape here for a little while. Let me deal with Bonny. She won't be *that* unreasonable."

"Then why would you want him—us—to go away?" Griff asked.

"To remove any temptation on her part," Fyre explained. "And, even though Artaxis might be reasonable, he was very angry about my brother and you being together before. He might not be as calm as you or Gia expect him to be."

"Well, Artaxis *has* always wanted Griff in the harem," Gia mused. "I suppose he might be a bit miffed."

"He wanted you in the harem?" Blaze sounded shocked and angry. "And he's banging your sister?"

"He's banging a lot of people," Gia declared. "It's his right as king, as long as all harem members are willing. No one is forced to be his."

"And we wouldn't be the only siblings in his harem." Griff frowned. "Or the only people related. I believe there are entire mature families in it." Wasn't there? He looked at Gia.

Gia nodded while Fyre and Blaze both muttered their non-approval of such things.

Before Gia and Fyre could get into any more squabbles, Griff tugged Blaze away from the other two. "I wanted you to leave with me. I've never done anything so spontaneous—that I can remember—as I have with you. Even when I was going to court another, I'd planned everything out."

"Court another?" Blaze narrowed his eyes.

"He seemed a safe, logical choice," Griff offered. "And I would have been miserable with him, and he with me. We certainly wouldn't have bonded."

"Well, duh. There's only one bond that could have happened for you, and I'm it." Blaze grinned, and caressed Griff's jaw. "So I guess I shouldn't be jealous, much."

"At all. Sometimes, I can almost see him, other times…most of the time, I forget how he looked completely. But I know this—he wasn't a fine, sexy man like you, with so much beautiful skin and freckles that make me want to—" He remembered they weren't alone and stopped himself from getting graphic. Griff settled for waggling his eyebrows at Blaze, which in turn got a deep gut-laugh from the man.

"I wanted you to run away with me, and help me find my wings," Griff said. "I want an adventure with you, and not one where there's an angry dragon queen trying to hurt you." He couldn't express the need to take off with Blaze, to have the man to himself. It was just there, and he hadn't forgotten it or changed his mind. "Gia can make a map for us. In case I forget where the incident occurred."

"You always do go to the wrong spot," Gia said from behind him.

Griff waited for Blaze to make up his mind. When the dragon smiled broadly, openly, Griff knew he was about to have an adventure indeed.

Chapter Seventeen

Blaze was pretty sure the dragonfly he was on was trying to kill him. Sweat dripped into Blaze's eyes as the evil creature took another stomach-quivering turn.

He'd thought it'd be fun, being shrunk down to mini-size along with Griff so they could both fly again...sort of. Griff's fairy magic was powerful enough to include Blaze, and the gods knew Blaze had been eager to be in the air again, even if it wasn't with his own wings.

But his dragonfly-mount was freakin' insane! The dips and turns were making Blaze want to upchuck.

Shadnay was being much nicer to Griff, who was flying a little in front of Blaze through the narrow openings in the foliage. Blaze knew he was being harassed purposely.

At least it was taking his mind off his worries in regards to Fyre and Bonny. Blaze couldn't think about anything but not falling off and splattering on the massive boulders — pebbles, if he'd been regular size — below.

When they stopped to give the buzzing beasts a break, Blaze's legs wobbled and he almost face-planted. The insides of his thighs ached in a truly not enjoyable way, and his ass was a tad sore — also not in a remotely enjoyable manner.

Griff wrapped an arm around Blaze's waist and stared at him, worry evident in those pretty lavender eyes. "Are you okay?"

Shadnay buzzed, and the other dragonfly did too. Blaze was certain they were laughing at him. "Oh yeah?" he muttered, glaring over his shoulder at them. "Well, fuck you, too." And now he'd get dumped for sure.

Griff stopped trying to get him to walk and instead twisted his torso around to look at the insects. "What did you two do?" The anger was barely concealed when he spoke. He cocked his head, and his lips thinned as he waited for an answer.

Blaze managed to keep back a gleeful cackle. The dragonflies were going to get scolded. It'd have taken a better man than him not to be glad of it, not when he'd apologized for his earlier mistake and he'd *really* been looking forward to being in the air again. That enjoyment had been snatched away from him by a psychotic bug.

Griff snapped, "Spit it out!"

Shadnay buzzed, then smacked the other dragonfly with his back end.

"Right," Griff sniffed. "I'm sure it was all Eleandross' fault, Shadnay. You didn't have *anything* to do with it."

Shadnay seemed agitated, flitting and bouncing in the air, and smacking Eleandross again.

Blaze wondered where in Hades the bugs got their names.

"Well, you might not have known he was doing it while we were in the air, but I heard you laugh at Blaze a minute ago, and that's unacceptable. We'll walk from here," Griff said. "It's not like we're far from the frolic proper anyway."

"Walking might be good," Blaze offered. "I'm not used to riding bu—er, anything else. M'kinda sore."

Griff ignored whatever Shadnay and Eleandross were buzzing on about and focused on Blaze. "Sore? I didn't even think." He looked around the area. "Aha! This might be soft enough…"

"Soft enough for what?" Blaze asked as Griff led him toward a lush little flowered spot.

"I was going to snap us back to standard size, but there's so little grass and natural cushioning here," Griff muttered.

As if trying to kiss ass—and they probably were—Shadnay and Eleandross swooped down to drop dandelion fluff on the spot Griff was leading them to.

"I'm still mad at you both," Griff informed the insects when he and Blaze had landed and shifted. He tugged Blaze's hand. "Lie down, and I'll work some of the soreness out of you. If we wait, it'll set in and make you miserable."

"It's not that bad," Blaze protested. "We were only on them for a few hours."

Griff pursed his lips and raised his eyebrows at Blaze.

"What?" Blaze asked, trying not to twitch under that appraising look.

"Are you saying you don't want my hands on you?"

Blaze sputtered. "What? No! No, did I *say* that? I don't think so! I—" *What in Hades am I arguing about?*

Blaze snapped his mouth shut and eased himself onto the padded makeshift bed. "Oh... oh gods, this is nice." Truthfully, he was sore inside, too, a lingering reminder of Bonny's temper.

"This *is* nice." Griff purred and caressed Blaze's back from shoulders to butt. "You really must be nude for a proper massage."

Blaze turned his head enough to see Griff out of one eye. "How about an improper one?" His dick twitched, his groin warming with arousal.

Griff snickered and pushed his hands up under Blaze's shirt. "I suppose there's no reason to hurry anywhere right now, is there?"

Blaze wiggled, trying to encourage Griff to take the shirt off him. "Nope, no reason to hurry at all—hey, wait a minute. Is that a roundabout way of telling me to have some patience here?"

"Do you know, when I'm with you, I feel so steady."

Blaze frowned, confused but happy by the statement. "Uh?"

"I know, that's quite the non-sequitur. Had nothing to do with what you said," Griff explained. "But it's the truth, and it's what's in my heart. I feel so lost so much of the time. Even when I'm remembering what I need to. It doesn't matter, because I know what happened to me. Most of the time, anyway. Sometimes I forget, I guess. But with you, I hardly think about what's wrong with me. I'm too busy thinking about *you*. It's wonderful. *You're* wonderful."

Blaze's skin heated all over with a blush. "I'm not. No one else thinks I am. I lost control once and burned a guy when we were...well, we didn't get that far, but it happened, the burning thing, and everyone thinks I'm a freak with no self-control even though I never lost control like that again. I mean sometimes I can't get my fire to work or it works when I—" Gods! He bit his tongue to stem the babbling. The metallic taste of his blood made his gut clench.

"Are you afraid you'll hurt me?" Griff asked.

"Can't. Bonny took my fire and shifting away." And for once, he was grateful for part of that, at least. He wouldn't be able to live with himself if he hurt Griff.

Griff did something, murmured a few quiet words, and Blaze was suddenly, gloriously naked. "You wouldn't hurt me even if you had your gifts back."

Blaze wasn't so certain. "Not intentionally, no, never. I can't control the fire. I've tried. I've trained with the masters. I've been, er, disciplined to encourage—"

Griff growled, and for a lithe fairy, he sounded very fierce. "Disciplined to encourage what?"

Blaze would have answered, but Griff chose that moment to grip the tops of Blaze's shoulders and squeeze. "Oh...oh gods." Blaze's eyes rolled. "Can we stop with the deep conversation and stick with the deep massage for now? Please? That feels so good."

"And I'm only just beginning," Griff murmured. "We'll get back to the subject we were discussing, but for now, I am going to make you feel very, *very* good."

Chapter Eighteen

Touching Blaze was so amazing that it was beyond anything Griff could have ever fantasized about. He was pretty sure that for a very long time he'd wanted someone just for him, all his own. Yes, he'd get glimmers of thoughts and memories, and he knew he'd been off to court someone when he'd gotten hurt.

But the yearning for a love all his own still swelled in him, and the gratitude and sheer appreciation he experienced anew every time he touched Blaze or even when Griff looked at him sometimes, was incredibly humbling. Griff had never expected to be bonded to anyone, much less someone as magnificent and big-hearted as Blaze. He knew, under the feisty shell the man wore, was a sweetness that Blaze wanted to keep hidden.

But Griff would get to see it, experience it, learn all the intricacies and nuances of Blaze in their shared lifetime.

So there, under the shade of the shrubs, with a light wind blowing, sending the leaves swaying and carrying the fragrant scent of spring blossoms to them, Griff fell completely for his bonded, his heart tumbling right into Blaze's hands.

He didn't mention it. The moment was so tender that he couldn't speak. Griff felt the warmth of Blaze's inner fire spreading into him, chasing off the last vestiges of frost that had been keeping that fragile organ sheltered.

Griff knelt beside his love, and when Blaze turned over, kissed him with a gentleness he'd never shared before, not with a lover. Blaze's lips parted on a moan, the warmth of his breath filling Griff and mingling with his.

Griff straddled Blaze, running his fingers through the silky orange strands of his hair, pushing them back so nothing impeded his view of Blaze's features. Griff traced the thick arched brows, the chiseled, stubbled cheeks. He took in Blaze's scent, the feel of him everywhere Griff touched.

Not just with his hands, but where his thighs, calves and ankles were pressed against Blaze, where his balls and ass rested on Blaze's groin.

He turned his head and rubbed his cheek over Blaze's, then arched to present his neck to the dragon.

Blaze shuddered, his breath sputtering out on a gasp as Griff wiggled, working up some friction between their lower halves.

Blaze held on to him, cupping Griff's buttocks and pulling him down harder. He opened his mouth against Griff's neck and nipped.

Griff couldn't even squeak as his body was suffused with pleasure. It shot out from every spot where he and Blaze touched.

Their clothes had long since been removed when Griff stretched out on top of Blaze, his legs framing the dragon's, their cocks nicely aligned. Griff couldn't stop kissing, touching, rubbing.

He wanted to feel every inch of Blaze, ached to bury his shaft deep into his bonded's body. Only the lack of proper lubricant held him back, and besides which, the slow, rolling thrusts they shared were scintillatingly erotic.

The freedom to linger over every touch, every kiss, was new for him and from Blaze had said about his past, for him too. It was evident how much Blaze was enjoying the luxury as well from the slow strokes of his hands on Griff and the soft moans, the guttural sounds the dragon made as the heat between them increased, their bodies slick with sweat, need enveloping them and blocking out everything else in the world.

Griff tried to keep his eyes open, but his lids were heavy. He undulated against Blaze, then hissed as he worked a hand between them.

Blaze rolled them onto their sides a moment later, and added one of his big, rough hands to their cocks too.

"Griff," Blaze mumbled, the name sounding thick, as if the dragon were intoxicated.

Griff tried to reply, to make a verbal acknowledgment, but sparks seemed to burst behind his closed lids, and he arched, thrusting harder.

The short jabs increased the ecstasy spiraling out from his dick. Griff let go of their shafts and instead grabbed on to Blaze. He tugged, and they went over again, this time with Griff on his back.

"Fuck. *Griff.*" Blaze said his name like a plea.

Griff felt feverish with lust, his balls tight and drawn up. He clutched at Blaze, curling his fingers against muscles and skin, marking his mate.

"Blaze," he got out, driving his hips up, needing more.

Blaze sat up, his ass on Griff's thighs.

Griff forced his eyes open, and his heart almost stopped when he saw Blaze, his orange hair disheveled, lips red and swollen, eyes glazed and nostrils flaring. Puffs of smoke left his nostrils, and his chest heaved with every inhalation and release.

Griff dragged the nails from one hand down Blaze's thigh, not breaking skin, but leaving streaks of pink behind on it.

Blaze shouted, bending over him. He let go of Griff's cock and instead jacked himself, his gaze locked with Griff's.

Griff used his other hand to fist his own shaft as well, and the orgasm that slammed into him took him by surprise. There were no warning flashes of heat, no rolling of his belly or tendrils of bliss.

It tore through him like a violent summer storm, the kind he loved to stand out in, letting the wind whip his hair and the rain pelt his skin. He had never felt so alive as he did then, or hadn't, until Blaze.

Blaze arched his back, his hand flying as he jacked his cock. It was an amazing sight to see, and Griff managed to use his spunk-splattered hand to rub at Blaze's tight balls.

The garbled yell Blaze loosed was followed by the first jet of his hot cum hitting Griff's lips and cheek. Griff licked, the pungent scent and briny taste drawing a moan from him.

He wanted to be covered in Blaze's cum, wanted it to coat his skin and soak into him. He wanted a deep, deep joining with Blaze, one that connected them on a cellular level.

Blaze shuddered and shook as he slowed his strokes, then eventually stopped. "Gods," he rasped, collapsing over Griff, catching himself on one broad hand.

Griff opened his mouth, intent on saying something, something *perfect* —

Only to snap his mouth shut as a mighty bellow demolished the sounds of his and Blaze's panted breaths.

Chapter Nineteen

"Ack!" Griff yelped, scampering to his feet.

Blaze was right there with him, trying to put himself between Griff and whatever monster was bellowing. Whatever it was, it hadn't shut up yet.

"What is it?" Blaze asked, backing up, pushing Griff with him. "Make me big!"

"Why? You can't shift or burn him! It!" Griff grabbed one of his arms. "Blaze, is that your evil queen?"

Blaze snorted, amused despite being freaked out. "No, no, it's not Bonny. She's not near as loud. That's...that's...ugh! I should know what makes that sound!"

Blaze turned to look at Griff. He got it, understood Blaze's frustration completely. Griff knew well, the anguish at not recognizing—or remembering—something he thought he should be able to remember. "Hey. It's okay. Let's just, oh, you know. Run!"

The ground began to shake with the impact of heavy footsteps, and yeah, Griff had brought up a damned good point. Blaze couldn't do much of anything to defend them. Whatever was coming their way was huge and sounded like it was pissed off beyond all measure.

At that moment, Shadnay and Eleandross swooped down and buzzed urgently. "Get on," Blaze ordered, lifting Griff, clutching at the fairy's narrow waist to hoist him onto Shadnay. "Go!" he shouted at the dragonfly.

"Blaze!" Griff looked panicked, but there was no need.

"I'm coming!" Blaze didn't hesitate to get on Eleandross's back, despite the earlier ride from Hades.

Naked on a dragonfly was *not* an erotic experience at all. There were fine, bristly hairs on Eleandross's back that were quite uncomfortable. Blaze was going to have prickly spots all over between his thighs and — he winced — his balls and ass.

The thundering footsteps grew louder, as did the yelling. Blaze twisted around, looking behind them to see what the fuck was coming their way.

"Oh…" He gulped, his eyes feeling huge and on the verge of popping right out of his head. "Shit!"

"What?" Griff yelled. "Shit!"

Griff must have turned around, Blaze figured. And he had to have seen the huge, scary as all get out creature ripping out trees and tossing them aside as though they were nothing.

But Blaze had to wonder why there was an angry orc in the area. And was it coming at them or what?

Large, very large, and the color of fresh green peas, the creature had fangs as long as Blaze's hand when he wasn't mini-sized. Small beady eyes were barely visible under the thick overhang of a brow, and the lumpy bald pate was glistening with sweat.

Snot dripped down the thing's face, barely noticeable considering the color.

And sweat streamed down its cheeks.

Wait. What's that? Blaze almost fell off Eleandross. Were those...*tears? Do orcs cry?* All Blaze knew about the ghastly beasts were that nine out of ten of them were male, and they had some weird customs no one was privy to...and they could kill without remorse, and often did.

None of those were reasons to hang around and see if the orc was crying or not.

"Go, go, go!" he shouted at the dragonflies.

But Griff was turning Shadnay around, and Blaze closed his eyes for a second to just take stock of what might be the last moments of his life. "Please tell me you're not going to—shit. You are."

Griff zipped past him on Shadnay. "Hey! Hey you!"

"Griff, that's an orc!" Blaze shouted. "Eleandross, come on." Blaze's heart pounded. Gods be damned, if he just had his powers back, he could maybe possibly just perhaps toast the orc. Although, their skin was really thick and probably roast-proof.

"Griff! No!" Blaze risked getting tossed off the dragonfly he was on, digging his heels against Eleandross's side. "Hurry up! Griff!"

What the heck was Griff doing? Blaze didn't know him well, that was true, but he knew Griff wasn't crazy.

No, he was a Love fairy, so why would he be going toward an orc—

"Oh, come on," Blaze whined, hoping he was wrong.

But with the continuous bellowing—which some might construe to be moans of agony—and the tears and snot... "Aw, shit!"

"Griff, come on." But Blaze felt it now, the same tug toward the ugly, pained orc. Sympathy, that's what it was. And a Love fairy would be inclined to help if someone…er, thing…had a broken heart, possibly.

Griff did hesitate, hovering with Shadnay while Blaze caught up to him.

Blaze held a hand up to Griff. "Please. Look at it. Him. It—whatever!"

"He," Griff said, gesturing, and that was when Blaze noted the complete lack of covering over the orc's genitals.

"Fuck." Blaze was equal parts horrified and, well, fascinated. "How can he walk with that thing?"

"Much less run," Griff added. "But can't you feel his pain? He's heartbroken, Blaze, not angry. He's hurting."

"How can you be so sure?" Blaze asked. "He could be crying and snotting because he's…he's…got gas. And if that's the case, we *really* need to get out of here."

Griff grimaced. "I feel it. I think we need to help him. At least talk to him."

"No, no, we don't." But as if the awful creature knew they were there, it slowed to a stop and sniffled.

Which was really gross. Blaze had never thought he had a sensitive stomach before then. "That's…that's disturbing," he muttered, watching the mucus stretch and pop back up to the orc's nose.

"Urk." Griff made another gagging sound, then gulped. "Er. He's looking at us, isn't he? I can't tell with that massive forehead."

"And eyebrow. He's just got the one, and yet...not a single hair on his head." Blaze patted his own thick locks and shuddered. "Maybe that's why he's upset."

Griff shot him a dirty look. "Stop it. He might hear you."

The orc cocked his head and made a clicking sound, rubbing his teeth together.

Blaze told himself he was *not* afraid. Clothes would have helped him believe it. Somehow, sitting nude astride a dragonfly made him feel very vulnerable.

The orc wiped his nose and flung the excess goop off his forearm. His bottom lip trembled, and a fat tear spilled down his cheek.

Blaze tried not to feel bad for the guy, but it was no use. "Shit."

"Exactly," Griff agreed. "Let me talk for a moment, okay?"

"Don't go any closer." It was the most Blaze could compromise.

"I won't." Griff sent him a sweet smile, then looked at the orc. "Do you speak, um, at all?"

The orc raised his head, his chins wobbling. "Of course I speak, quite well, thank you. I'm not quite the oaf I appear to be."

Blaze bit his tongue to keep from commenting that he was sure as shit acting like an oaf, hollering and tearing up the forest.

But the orc sighed, his fetid breath reaching them. Blaze wasn't the only one who gagged.

"Could you just...not?" he asked, fanning the air away from his face.

The orc seemed to droop, his massive shoulders rounding. He canted his head down. "Sorry. I haven't been able to clean myself up since being purged from my pack."

"Purged?" Griff asked. "Like…like banned?"

"Exactly that, except of course I'll be put down if I return." The orc shrugged. "And so I'm alone in the world now, with the most broken of hearts."

"Oh, gods," Blaze groaned quietly, knowing there was no chance he and Griff would be zipping away now.

"The most broken of hearts?" Griff repeated, nudging Shadnay forward.

Blaze was glad Eleandross followed suit.

"Yes," the orc said. "Forgive me. I am Grlind."

"I'm Griff, and this is my bonded, Blaze." When Griff smiled at him with so much affection, Blaze knew he'd face a hundred orcs for the fairy.

"Bonded?" Grlind sniffled again and scrubbed at his cheeks as tears poured from his eyes. "That is…everything I-I w-wanted, but we can't—"

"Shit." Blaze looked the orc over. Really, Grlind wasn't but maybe a foot taller than him in Blaze's standard man-size. Of course, Grlind had about a hundred pounds on him, at least, but Blaze had seen him running. The orc wasn't faster than him, or faster than Griff.

"Can you make us regular size?" Blaze asked Griff.

Griff nodded. "Grlind, we're going to do a little magic here. Please don't be startled."

"You're a fairy," Grlind observed. "But where are your wings?"

Blaze hissed at him. "Stop asking questions!"

"It's fine," Griff said. "They were knocked off in an attack that reached through the veil. And it also screwed up my brain."

"Reached through the veil? But that isn't possible," Grlind protested.

"Do you see any wings?" Blaze snapped. "And I'm a dragon who can't shift or use my fire." Oh, maybe he shouldn't have given that information up. He'd just exposed their vulnerable belly, so to speak.

But Grlind shrugged. "I'm not a violent orc, hence my current status. I refused to kill one too many times."

"How many times did you refuse to kill in total?" Blaze asked.

"Just the once," Grlind said. "It was enough. I've killed in defense before, but I would not help annihilate a village just so our pack could have the gold. And here I am, outcast, with my lover among those who voted for me to be in such a state. He even cast the first stone."

"Cast the first stone?" Blaze had heard stories about the orcs, but he had no true knowledge of the creatures.

"Yes. When one is purged, outcast, he—I was stripped of all my belongings, then chased from our pack while being pelted with stones. It is often the fate of the purged one to die before he ever makes his way free," Grlind explained. A sad expression flitted over his face. "I've no doubt that would have been the better fate for me."

"Oh, don't say that!" Griff exclaimed. "I know how sorrow feels, how it is to dislike yourself." He got off Shadnay as soon as the dragonfly lowered him close to the ground.

Blaze dismounted Eleandross a second later, then both dragonflies flitted up and out of reach. "Griff, you are only loveable, always. Eminently." Gods, he hoped that was the right word. It sounded right in his head.

Griff just glowed for him, smiling so brightly. "Thank you, Blaze. The same is true for you."

Grlind sighed. "I'll never have that, what you two have. Orcs don't have bonded mates, and—and we aren't to love a man of our kind. Have sexual relations with one, yes. There are so few females, but love one? It isn't done. Another rule I broke, falling for my lover." He shook his head, and the tears started again before he covered his face with his hands.

Griff chanted, and he and Blaze were taller in an instant.

"You don't know what the future holds," Griff said to the orc. "Look at us. A dragon and a fairy, bonded. Have you ever heard such a thing?"

Grlind peeked out from between his fingers. "But both of you are beautiful, and nude. I am a hideous thing. Even our female orcs don't want to have sex with us, but no one else will have sex with *them*, and so it goes."

Blaze had to agree about the ugly part, but he had enough sense not to say as much. That, and Griff squeezed his hand hard, so he knew to keep his opinion to himself.

"I'm just going to run until I die," Grlind said after a moment. "What point is there to living?"

"Wow," Blaze snapped. Had he ever wallowed in so much self-pity? *Maybe.* "You are a whiny baby. Cut it out and stop feeling sorry for yourself."

"Blaze!" Griff tried to snatch his hand away, but Blaze brought it to his lips and kissed the back of Griff's knuckles.

"It's true, and he needs to hear it." Blaze cut his eyes toward Grlind. "You're all ready to die—so why did you even run, Grlind? Why not let them stone you to death?"

Grlind blinked. "I…I d-don't know."

Blaze did. "Because you don't want to die. You just hurt inside right now, but you don't want to die."

"But there's no place for me out here." Grlind gestured to the world in general, Blaze supposed. "None. Orcs stick together, unless we're hired out to perform a task. We keep to ourselves even then. I don't know how to not be a part of a pack. I —"

"You just need to relax," Blaze advised. "And you're not alone." Ugh, he was a moron. But when he looked at Griff, there was such obvious approval in those lovely eyes of his, Blaze felt like a hero. And for that, he'd continue with his offer. "You can come with us. We're on a quest."

"A quest?" Grlind perked up. "A noble one? I've never been on a noble quest. Just paid ones. Is it a noble one? Tell me it is!"

Gods, the orc was as excited as a baby dragon begging for lava treats.

"It's a very noble one," Griff said firmly. "To find my wings and see if there's a rip in the veil."

"Oh! There must be! The veil is supposed to be impenetrable," Grlind said. "Are you sure that's what happened?"

Blaze let Griff tell the story, and he listened closely, as he always did to Griff.

But Blaze began to wonder exactly what had happened when Griff was harmed. A rip in the veil seemed so unbelievable an occurrence. He'd never heard of it happening before, ever.

Magical creatures could cross over into the boring real world if they were powerful enough. That was true, and on occasion a mage or witch or even an elf managed to go over. They came back powerless, if they came back at all.

So how could the veil have been breached from the other side?

Or had it been?

Chapter Twenty

Originally, Griff had intended to take Blaze to the frolic lands and spend at least one night in his own home.

Adding an orc to the mix — a naked orc at that — put a kibosh on Griff's plan. For one thing, he didn't know enough about orcs to judge whether or not Grlind could be trusted.

Secondly, he had nowhere to put the orc in the frolic. Grlind wasn't a giant — everyone knew giants were dangerous — giants never tried to keep that a secret — but he was still much, much taller than Griff and a lot more muscle-y. Griff also didn't think Egregio would care for the orc at all, and Griff didn't want the monster suffocating Grlind in his sleep or anything like that.

"We need to find something to cover *that* up with," Blaze griped, pointing at Grlind's obnoxiously huge cock. "I'm beginning to feel lacking."

They'd put their clothing back on already. Griff patted Blaze's butt. "You are perfect. Grlind's shaft is frightening." It was another area where Grlind was much bigger than he was.

The orc wasn't close enough to hear them, having stopped to try and replant the tree he'd almost ripped from the ground. Most of the others Grlind had smacked, as far as Griff could see, had been snapped in half, not pulled up.

Blaze wrinkled his nose. "Yeah, that's too much of a good thing. Which, that makes it a bad thing, right?" He shrugged. "Whatever. I don't want to see that thing flopping all over. But you know what?" He looked at Griff, appearing to be quite pleased with himself.

"What?" Griff asked, smiling back automatically. He couldn't be unhappy when Blaze looked so happy himself.

"I *finally* understand what the word *pendulous* means!" Blaze chuckled. "But, damn. Imagine that pecker hard. Think it'd stand out straight, or —"

"I'd prefer not to muse on Grlind's penis," Griff said. And maybe figuring out a way to cover that appendage up, as well as Grlind's *pendulous* balls, would be a great idea that should be implemented immediately. Griff cast about for something he could use just for that purpose.

Shadnay buzzed, chattering at him. Eleandross dipped and bobbed around Shadnay.

"What're the bugs saying?" Blaze ducked a dive-bomb from Eleandross. "Dragonflies! Insects! I didn't think bugs was an insult!"

Griff saw the teasing glint in Blaze's eyes, the twitch of his lips. The dragon was getting a kick out of riling the bugs — *er, insects* — up.

Blaze's smile was astoundingly real. There was no other way to describe it. He was *happy*, and part of that was Griff hoped, because of him.

Griff stood on his toes and reached for Blaze. He had to taste that smile, or he'd just die.

Blaze tasted like sunshine and joy, like love and fun and sex. Griff moaned softly, slipping his tongue deeper into Blaze's mouth. He moved his hands down to cup Blaze's firm ass and gave both cheeks a squeeze.

He loved the way Blaze moved closer, the press of his hardening cock through their clothing, the heave of his chest. Griff wanted to just—

"Oh. Er. I could leave?"

Griff groaned and stopped kneading Blaze's ass. He'd probably given Grlind quite the show.

"Sorry," Griff whispered to Blaze, in case he was embarrassed.

But that huge, sweet smile was still on Blaze's face. "It's good. So good."

After a moment, they separated, and Blaze turned to face Grlind. "Man, you have *got* to do something with that thing."

Grlind looked confused for a second, then he smirked. "What? Like heft it over my shoulder?"

Griff snorted while Blaze laughed.

Grlind jostled the body part currently being discussed. "I might need it to prop myself up on when we take a break. After all, I'll be walking."

"What do you know?" Blaze asked. "Your cock's almost as big as your ego!" He laughed again, and Grlind did, too.

"There's no almost to it." Grlind stopped waving his prick and looked around. "There! I'm handy with weaving and braiding. I can use that vine, although, if the leaves wilt... Can't you magic me some clothing, Griff?"

If he could remember the chant for it, Griff could have done so, but his mind blanked when he tried.

And Griff's amusement morphed into frustration. He turned away from the orc and Blaze. "No, I can't."

There was a moment of silence, then Grlind said, "That's okay. Don't feel bad, Griff. I think we've all felt bad enough in our lives already. I'll braid the vine into thick strands. We orcs are handy like that."

Blaze took Griff's hand, and startled Griff by raising it and kissing Griff's palm. "He's right. No dwelling on anything that makes us sad or angry. Not today, and tomorrow, we'll set the same rule, just for that day, and so we'll go until we're past what hurts us."

Griff didn't know if that would work for him. Not if he never found his wings. His memory, that he could maybe deal with, but the inability to fly was crippling him in more ways than one.

Even so, he could bury his pain for his bonded. Griff nodded. "Okay." Grlind trudged off to the vine he'd pointed at. "And we'll keep an eye out for some perunian flowers. You know the ones, purple and gold with orange leaves?" *That* he could remember, thank the gods.

Blaze frowned. "I don't think so."

Grlind was close enough that he heard Griff shout the same question at him.

"Yes, I know of it. It's what we orcs use for—" He smirked at them. "*Personal relations.*"

"Personal relations?" Blaze scowled. "What the fuck?"

"Well, not just personal, because if there's more than just this involved"—Grlind waved his left hand at them—"that plant comes in handy. Heh. Handy."

"Good gods, our orc friend is our dork friend," Blaze said, eyes rounding. "Who'd have guessed?"

Griff was tempted to thump Blaze for the bad pun, but instead, he kissed him. It was a fierce, brief kiss that left Blaze panting and trying to get more.

Griff murmured against his wet lips, "*Lube*, my mate. The stalks of the plant produce a viscous liquid that makes the best sexual lubricant."

Chapter Twenty-One

Perunian. Huh. It's kind of ugly. But Blaze could sure deal with ugly if it meant getting lube, then getting fucked. "Is this it?" he asked, reaching for the orange-leafed flower.

"What—Blaze! No!" Griff shouted.

Too late, because Blaze already had his hand closing around the plant and while he heard the alarm in Griff's voice—hard not to, the way he shrieked—Blaze couldn't get the command not to grab, sent from his brain to his hand, to follow through in time to stop his motion.

So he screamed like a dragon getting his scales ripped off as pain exploded throughout his hand and forearm. He couldn't even get his hand to work so he could jerk it away from the damned plant.

"Blaze!" Griff was right there, pulling at his arm, gripping his elbow and panting as he gave a mighty tug. "Let go of the flower!"

"Oy, that's gonna hurt," Grlind said. "You forgot about the purple and gold petals. That's got purple and white petals, and it's got these fine poisonous fibers on it. Paralyzes what touches it, at least for a few hours."

"Fuck!" Blaze's vision blurred as his eyes rolled. "I hate pain. *Hate it!*"

Grlind looked at Griff. "On the count of three, you pull again while I get the flower. As thick-skinned as I am, it won't hurt me like it does him."

"Are you sure?" Griff asked, panting slightly as he clung to Blaze.

"Pretty sure." Grlind shrugged. "We've got quite thick skins. Not like scales, but tough enough. So let's give this a go. One, two, three!" He reached down and swatted the whole flower aside, while Griff pulled hard enough to send Blaze and him both tumbling backward.

Grlind grabbed them and shoved them to the side. "More of the flowers," he explained, shaking out the hand he'd used on the evil flower. "But where these are, the perunian is usually nearby."

"Not sure it's worth risking," Blaze muttered. "What if the flowers have mutated? I'm going to have nightmares about this plant for weeks." He looked at his hand. His palm was dark red, his hand swollen, as was half his forearm. "Is this shit going to kill me?" he asked around a ball of fear he was trying to suppress.

"No, it'll be fine after a few hours," Griff said, taking Blaze's hand and looking it over. "I'm sorry. I didn't think about poisonous plants. I mean, I..." He scrunched up his nose. "I think I know which ones are poisonous, but what if I don't? What if I remember wrong and it gets you hurt?"

"Here now," Grlind said. "I'll grab the plants from now on. It's the least I can do since you have both let me accompany you."

Blaze wasn't arguing. "How's your hand?"

Grlind held it up. It was just big, period. "Barely stung."

"Well, fuck you," Blaze groused.

Grlind's beady eyes widened, then he guffawed, and it scared the nearby tree sprites out of their homes. They shot up and away like a swirling, whistling mass of pastel colors, chattering and scolding as they fled.

"Oops. Pretty little things," Grlind observed.

"My hand's going to fall off," Blaze said. He couldn't even wiggle his fingers.

Griff shook his head. "No, it won't." He sniffed the air. "There's a river to the south of us. Soaking your hand would help."

Blaze whimpered. "That'd be awesome. It hurts." So he whined a little. He was allowed to, considering how much pain he was in.

"Grlind, we are heading to the river to soak Blaze's hand," Griff said. "Are you coming?"

"I'll meet you there," Grlind said. "I'm just going to pick that perunian for you. It's right there."

"Okay. Join us when you're done here?" Griff waited until Grlind agreed, then he and Blaze headed to the river.

And all Blaze could think about was the perunian and what could happen once Griff had enough lube.

Blaze had never, ever wanted something like he wanted Griff's cock in him. *Gods help anything that tries to get in the way of that happening tonight*, Blaze thought.

No offense intended. I'm not tempting Fate or anything. I'm just… I'll beg for some alone time with my bonded and some lube tonight. Please, please be kind enough to let us have that.

At the river, Blaze could have wept with relief when he dipped his hot hand into the water. He sat there with Griff, and eventually, Grlind, until his hand stopped throbbing.

Once the swelling was almost gone and the pain was more of a bad memory than a reality, Blaze was ready to get going.

He had plans for Griff, and judging by the heated looks Griff kept sending his way, Griff had plans of his own.

Since Grlind was smirking and holding a bouquet of flowers *almost* identical to the one Blaze had grabbed, Blaze figured the orc had picked up on the sexual tension between Blaze and Griff.

Even the dragonflies were more buzzy than usual. Blaze wondered if they were going to have a few peepers tonight.

Chapter Twenty-Two

"I can't believe our luck," Blaze griped. "Actually, yeah, I can." He kept muttering as they sought shelter from the chilling downpour.

Griff tried to keep his teeth from chattering, but it was *cold*! Shadnay and Eleandross had long since flitted off to escape the rain and wind. Griff couldn't blame them one bit for not hanging back.

Grlind stopped and gestured toward some dark shape Griff couldn't make out. "What?" Had Grlind even heard him in the ruckus of the storm?

"Let me go check it out and make certain it's safe," Grlind shouted.

Blaze pressed close to Griff. "Cave. There's a cave. I don't care if there's a family of trolls in there — we're going in and getting out of this shitty weather!"

Griff didn't think they were all that far from the path he'd been on when he'd been hurt. Then again, who knew if he was right? *Blaze will know.* "You still have the map Gia gave you?"

"It's in the pack. Grlind has it," Blaze answered.

Griff frowned. Had he asked that already?

Before he could fret over it, Grlind was calling for them, which Griff assumed meant the cave was safe.

Even if it wasn't, Griff thought it might just be worth the risk of having to fight for the cave. He was soaking wet, cold and hungry.

The cave was very, very dark. Griff tried to pull up the spell for fire and panicked when he didn't immediately remember it. Then it came to him, and he murmured the words that kindled a small, vibrant flame.

"I could have done that once upon a time," Blaze muttered. "Um. Well, I probably would have burned everyone trying to do it, but I could have made fire eventually."

"Here's your pack. Good thing you didn't leave it tiny-sized and on a dragonfly," Grlind observed. "You'd both be out of luck."

"Out of luck?" Griff got the small fire settled on the ground and charmed it to remain burning. "What do you mean?"

Grlind smirked at him. "Are you forgetting what I picked for you earlier?"

Griff's cheeks burned and he focused on increasing the size of the fire. "Er. This cave is…" Gods, his voice echoed in it, and the echo didn't sound far off. "Small?"

"That it is." Grlind didn't look like he saw that as a bad thing.

Griff peeked at Blaze.

Blaze was staring at the pack Grlind had set down.

"I will go out to fetch our meal," Grlind said in a merry voice. "This weather is nothing for me, but you two are delicate."

"Delicate?" Blaze huffed, eyes snapping with irritation.

Griff opened the pack and pulled out one of the perunian flowers. "Blaze?"

Blaze had opened his mouth, his attention on Grlind. He turned to look at Griff instead. "Shit! Keep that away from me!"

Grlind chortled. "I'll take my time hunting up supper."

Griff barely heard the orc. His heart was pounding, his pulse racing, and all he heard was Blaze's sharp inhalation.

There, with the magical flame illuminating Blaze's features, Griff reached for his bonded.

Griff pulled Blaze closer, until there was little space between them. He covered Blaze's face with kisses before sealing their mouths together.

Need swamped him, filling him up with an urgent, sensual throbbing that he felt in every particle of his being.

And Blaze melted against him, leaning in, pressing that strong, sexy body to Griff's leaner form.

Griff ran his hands all over Blaze, working his clothes off while doing so. Griff's tunic was gone with a brush of Blaze's hands, then there was nothing between them, just the perfection of skin on skin.

Griff couldn't sink his tongue in deep enough, couldn't touch enough of Blaze's body to satisfy him. He growled and pushed and pulled until he had Blaze on the ground, spreading his legs, moaning and offering himself fully to Griff.

Slow down! Slow down! I'm a Love fairy. I'm better at sex than this! Because, *gods*, he wanted to just slick Blaze's hole up and shove right in. The need to be in Blaze, to lay claim to him in such an elemental way, and to give of himself all that he could — it was nearly over-powering.

But Griff slowed down, kissing Blaze with more tenderness than force. He savored instead of plundered, and the way Blaze reacted, the sweet sounds he made, the sensual undulations and loving touches were Griff's reward.

Had he continued to rush, he'd have missed so much. Griff nuzzled Blaze's cheek, then licked his jaw, his neck, sucked salty skin and left his mark behind.

All the while, he caressed every part of Blaze he could reach. The swell and curves of his biceps, the ridges of muscles and ribs, the fuzzy sides of Blaze's thighs.

Then there was the hard, wet-tipped cock that burned like a brand alongside Griff's. He thrust and thrust, pleasure building between them, flowing from Griff to Blaze, from Blaze to Griff.

It was beautiful and erotic, the scents and sounds, the feel and tastes they shared.

Griff moaned when Blaze nibbled on his Adam's apple. He whimpered when Blaze began to play with his nipples. Griff rolled them onto their sides and hitched one leg up, propping it on Blaze's waist.

He rubbed, back and forth, writhing and panting as Blaze pleasured him.

Then he pushed Blaze onto his back again and started seducing Blaze all over again. He nipped and licked Blaze's lips, his nipples, his ridged abs. He buried his nose in the bright orange pubic hair, thick and springy around Blaze's cock.

"My favorite place," he murmured.

Blaze's abs rippled as he curled up to look at him. "Could your favorite place be seven and a half inches up? Please?"

Griff snorted, fisting the base of Blaze's cock. "Eager?"

"Beyond," Blaze groaned, wiggling his hips. "You're going to fuck me, right?"

"I'm going to make love to you," Griff corrected gently, before rubbing his lips over the fat middle of Blaze's shaft.

"Same thing," Blaze rasped.

"Not at all," Griff informed him. "And I'll show you the difference."

"I—ohhhhhh," Blaze moaned as Griff licked the underside of his cock. "Oh, oh gods…oh—Griff!"

Yes, having the head of one's cock sucked into a perfectly tight, wet mouth tended to bring on a shout. Griff would have smiled had his mouth not been stretched and filled.

He moved his hands down to cup Blaze's ass and pushed.

Blaze got the message, moaning again as he pulled his legs up to his chest.

And Griff went on his most seductive path ever, losing himself in Blaze, not worrying about coming or doing anything other than bringing so much pleasure to Blaze that the man couldn't hold back.

Griff lapped his cock, taking it deep into his throat. At the same time, he rubbed his thumbs over Blaze's hole repeatedly. He didn't push in, not without the lubricant. He'd have to find the flower in a minute.

For now, he was content to suck and rub, and Blaze was certainly enjoying it. He was loud with his praise and pleas. Griff wanted to devour him, but he released Blaze's shaft, and rolled him onto his belly.

Griff tapped Blaze's hip. "Raise your butt."

"Urk," Blaze replied.

Griff grabbed the pack, then helped Blaze raise up enough so Griff could tuck it under his hips. "Beautiful." Griff stroked Blaze's luscious buttocks, admiring the shape of them — round and plump — as well as the light sheen of orange-gold hairs. With the firelight, Blaze's skin glowed, and Griff had to taste.

He kneaded Blaze's butt, squeezing, releasing, learning the texture and reactions of Blaze's rump.

Then he leaned down and ran his tongue from the top of Blaze's crack to his asshole.

"Griff!" Blaze yelped, shoving up onto his elbows.

Griff let go of one buttock and slid his hand up to press down on Blaze's back, between his shoulder blades.

Blaze went down again with a moan. He wiggled his ass and canted it up.

Griff pressed his face into that warm crevice, sniffing, licking, laving. Blaze writhed and squirmed, humping the pack. His hole gradually softened, that muscle giving way so Griff could push his tongue inside.

Blaze's shout bounced off the cave walls. Griff raised his head long enough to shove his hands under Blaze and tug, encouraging him to lift up.

Blaze came up onto his hands and knees. Griff fondled his balls and cock as he dipped his head back down, seeking out that little pucker once again.

When Blaze began to make answering thrusts, Griff used saliva to slip one finger into that tight, gripping heat. He had to feel around with the other hand until he located the flower. Luckily, he found it quickly.

Kneeling behind Blaze, Griff watched his finger, watched the way Blaze's hole closed tight around it. Griff bent and licked that wrinkled skin while he fingered Blaze, and when Blaze started babbling, Griff sat up again and withdrew his finger from Blaze's ass.

The plaintive whine from Blaze echoed the one Griff managed to stifle. He needed to prepare Blaze so they could join. "I'll be in you soon," Griff vowed.

He thought Blaze tried to say please, but Griff's brain kind of shorted out when Blaze reached underneath himself and tried to finger his own hole.

Griff growled and ripped open the stalk of the flower. The thick, creamy fluid gleamed like a beacon. Griff scooped out a good amount and spread it over his aching shaft. The next scoop went over Blaze's hole.

"Griff," Blaze whimpered, arching his lower back deeply.

Griff gritted his teeth and pushed two fingers in slowly, opening Blaze's ass up again. The lubricant was doing its job, increasing the arousal and smoothing the way for Griff to penetrate Blaze.

When Griff had his digits in far enough, he crooked them and rubbed over Blaze's gland.

Blaze cursed and glared over his shoulder. "Now, Griff. Now! I won't break!"

But Griff was in control, and he wanted to blow Blaze's mind. He twisted his fingers around, pulled them free, then began slipping a third one in.

Blaze mewled, and his eyes rolled as he lowered his head back onto his forearms.

Griff watched his fingers going in and out. He watched Blaze's expression, the bunching of his shoulders, the rolling of his hips.

And when he massaged Blaze's gland until Blaze was gasping and his cock dripping, Griff knew it was time. He gave Blaze's inner walls one more caress, then eased his fingers out and lined his cock up. "*Now.*"

Griff pushed his shaft into the most perfect, heated grip he'd ever experienced. The connection between him and Blaze swelled and pulsed as Griff sank in deeper and deeper.

When he was buried to the hilt in Blaze's ass, Griff could hardly breathe, the pleasure was so great. His vision blurred, and he curled over Blaze.

He peppered Blaze's neck and shoulders with kisses while Blaze panted, his ass gripping and rippling around Griff's cock.

Then some of that strangling grip loosened, and Griff began to move.

But he needed more. He needed to see Blaze's face fully, needed to feel Blaze's heart beating underneath him.

Griff threw his head back for a few more thrusts then pulled out carefully.

"No!" Blaze yelped.

"I want to see your face," Griff rasped. "Please."

Blaze's cheeks carried a pretty blush when he rolled over. That pink color spread down to Blaze's chest as Griff repositioned himself between Blaze's legs.

"Like this," Griff whispered, urging Blaze to hold on.

Blaze wrapped his legs around Griff's hips. "Kiss me."

Griff kissed Blaze as he pushed back into him, loving him with tongue and cock, heart and soul.

And Griff kept kissing him, rolling his hips, slowly filling Blaze over and over again. Never had he felt anything like the pleasure he experienced with Blaze.

Blaze kept trembling, moaning, kissing him eagerly. He gave everything, and Griff reveled in it, returned that devotion.

Need built until it had to take over. Griff moved faster, his kisses became rougher, his grip harder.

Blaze held on to him tightly and met him thrust for thrust. He nipped and bit at Griff's lips and tongue, losing control just as Griff was doing.

Griff had to break the kisses so he could push up and drive into Blaze harder. He loved the way Blaze arched his neck, his mouth opening on a long moan as Blaze fisted his own dick.

He was a picture of erotic perfection. Griff pinched Blaze's left nipple, and Blaze's ass clamped tight around Griff's cock. A second pinch, a twist, and Blaze shouted, eyes closing as cum spurted from his cock.

Griff's vision blurred, his ears buzzed as if a hive of bees had moved into them, and the rapturous climax that rolled through him was unlike any he could remember having before.

It seemed to go on and on as Blaze's ass milked his shaft. Griff might have yelled—he might have cursed or praised or sang for all he knew. His throat ached by the time his arms gave out, and he collapsed, shivering, sweaty and shaken to his core in a way he never wanted to be free of.

He managed, eventually, to move to lie beside Blaze. His cock had softened by then, and it slipped out.

"Ungh. So weird coming out," Blaze mumbled. "Tickles." He raised one leg and touched his hole. "Oh. That's...um. Wet?"

Griff snorted. He started to reply, opening his eyes —

But stopped when a pair of yellow eyes glowed back at him from the darkness beyond them.

Chapter Twenty-Three

"What the fu—" Blaze scrambled to his feet, seeing the odd yellow eyes at the same time Griff did. Warm seed trickled down his thighs and made it really hard for him not to squirm. "Come out and fight like a man!" he bellowed, raising his fisted hands.

"No, no fighting," Griff said. "No fighting."

Those yellow eyes blinked, and the pupils slitted from round to thin vertical lines barely wider than a blade of grass.

It was fucking creepy. Blaze raised his hands a little higher.

Griff tried to step in front of him.

Blaze wasn't having that. Whatever had the weird eyes had to be dangerous. Didn't it? "I've got this, Griff."

Griff slanted him a look that would have made Blaze back down had he not been worried his bonded would be hurt.

But before he could argue, something very much like a purr sounded, and a form stepped out of the darkness.

A naked, female form with all the curvy, bouncy bits. "Fight like a man?" she asked, her pointed ears twitching where they stuck out of her black hair. There was some sort of markings on her forehead, centered slightly above the space between her eyebrows. "If you really want a challenge, why not have me fight like a woman?"

There were more markings on the woman's shoulders and hips. Blaze wrinkled his nose at her. "With hair-pulling and lightning bolts?" He was being sarcastic and regretted smarting off immediately.

The woman wrinkled her nose right back at him. "You *are* a barbarian, but if you insist."

Griff gasped, but Blaze was too busy trying to figure out where in Hades he'd lost his damned mind, because the woman blurred and she wasn't a woman anymore. Now a tall, lean male—a very naked male with all the dangly bits—stood in the woman's place.

Blaze was so freakin' confused.

The man blinked lazily at him, then raised one hand and made a weird gesturing motion.

Griff stopped sounding like he was struggling for breath. "You're a...you're a..." He scowled and slapped a fisted hand against his palm. "Argh!"

One thin black eyebrow arched up the now-man's high forehead.

Blaze realized the face hadn't changed at all, just the gender of the body attached to it. He barely had enough sense to keep from asking something rude, like what the devils was the creature? After all, he'd already stepped in a pile of dragon dung during the whole *fight like a man* thing.

And he needed to comfort Griff. The fairy was agitated, muttering about how his brain didn't work right.

"Griff, it's okay," Blaze said, choosing to focus on his bonded. "I don't know what he is either." He went with the gender being exhibited and hoped he didn't screw up by doing so.

But the strange man nodded slightly and murmured, "Very good. There's hope for you yet."

Blaze was *not* flattered by that faint praise. He reached for Griff and pulled him into his arms. "It's okay. You'll remember. Or maybe you never knew what he was to begin with."

Griff shook his head. "No, I do. I did! It's right there on the edge of my memory, and it's *important*, I know it is! Argh!"

"What's the ruckus?" Grlind hollered from outside the cave. "I've got dinner. Are you two done bumping uglies?"

"Bumping uglies. How quaint," the stranger said.

Blaze ignored that. "We have company, Grlind."

Grlind came storming in, shaking off water from the storm and sending it flying everywhere. He held several bloody animal carcasses in one hand and some kind of plants in the other. "Was I wrong about a critter sheltering here?" Then he stopped, the firelight casting an eerie glow on his features. "What the fuck?"

"Exactly what I wondered," Blaze said. "He was a woman first."

"Would you prefer a name?" the stranger asked. "You may call me His Highness, unless I decide to transform into my feminine side. Then of course, I am Her Highness."

"How about we just call you That Annoying Stuck-Up Creep?" Blaze suggested.

"I'll settle for Jade, if the title is too long for your little brain to remember."

Griff remained silent, but Grlind took another step forward, almost walking directly into the fire. "Jade... Would you be the Storm King?"

Jade rolled his eyes. "*Finally* someone who knows their elven royalty."

"Storm King?" Blaze blinked. Even *he* had heard of the Storm King. He was powerful and weird and an elf. Elves weren't as common as some people thought they were anymore. Not after all the in-fighting of the last millennia.

Jade's full lips curled up into a smirk. "Unless, of course, I choose to alter forms." Which he did.

"Oh gods, there you go with the weird again," Blaze whined.

Jade cupped one breast and jiggled it. "Have you something against females?"

"No!" Blaze protested. "Whatever, whoever — It's the whole, BOOM! I'm a man! POOF! I'm a woman! That's what's freaking me out!"

"Why does the woman get the poof?" Jade asked.

Blaze smacked himself on the forehead.

"That's right," Griff said excitedly. "Elves are very progressive. They know no gender inequality."

"Whichever gender I am tends to be the superior one, so I wouldn't say you are correct," Jade sniffed. With a snap, she had her body covered in long robes. For all Blaze knew, she might not be female under them. He was going to get dizzy trying to keep track of her changes, so he decided not to bother trying.

And why was Grlind still standing close enough to the fire to scorch his skin? *Oh. That's right. His skin is thick.* Even so, Blaze hated the stench of burned flesh unless it was his dinner being cooked.

"Grlind, could you maybe move away from the fire?"

Jade made that purring noise again and flipped her hair over one narrow shoulder. "My beauty has entranced him."

Grlind's face went dark, which Blaze supposed was a blush. "An orc would know better than to be entranced by the likes of you, Storm King. You've annihilated entire villages at your whim. Floods, lightning, hail, whatever you chose to rain down on innocents."

Jade widened her eyes. "So you choose to believe." She looked back at Blaze and Griff. "I did enjoy watching you being taken by the fairy. A surprise, indeed, as I'd thought a dragon shifter would be the dominant one."

Griff spun around to face Jade. "It's not about dominance. We are bonded."

"Bonded?" There went that black eyebrow again. "Impossible. There is no interspecies bonding."

"Looks like you aren't the smarty-pants you thought you were," Blaze said. He felt back on solid footing then. "We *are* bonded. So there." He almost stuck his tongue out for added emphasis.

Jade canted her head and glanced at Griff. "In that case, my sympathies, little fairy."

Chapter Twenty-Four

Eventually, Griff was able to extract from his memory the information he'd been reaching for. The Storm King was elven royalty, and elves were one of the few species that were more sexually promiscuous than Love fairies. It was the royal blood that made the Storm King able to switch genders, and he was often referred to as the Storm Queen as well. Griff felt better having remembered, and he resumed listening to the elf talk.

"It's just a tedious little uprising," Jade said, having shifted back to his male form. "Nothing for me to be truly worried over."

"But you're hiding out in a cave," Blaze pointed out. "If you weren't worried over it, truly or otherwise, why hide?"

Jade sniffed and picked at something on his robes. "I am *not* hiding out. I am *communing with nature*, which is very important for us elves to do. Not that I'd expect a misogynistic dragon shifter to know that."

Blaze leapt up from where he'd been sitting by the fire. "I am not misotg—mistygen—mis—I'm not whatever that means!" he shouted, flinging his hands up in the air.

Jade chuckled snidely. "You don't even know what it means."

"Don't be an ass," Griff muttered. Royalty or not, powerful or not, the Storm King wasn't going to mock Blaze.

Jade blinked, then narrowed his eyes at Griff.

Griff braced for an insult or possibly a magic attack.

Instead, Jade smiled suddenly and waved the whole tense moment off. "So defensive of your...bonded. It's sweet."

Jade still didn't sound like he believed in the bonding, but Griff didn't care. It wasn't his job to convince anyone of it. He and Blaze knew it was real.

Blaze sat back down beside Griff and leaned his head close.

"He accused you of hating women," Griff explained quietly while Jade talked about himself.

Blaze huffed, his breath hot against Griff's ear. "I don't hate women!" He sat up and glared at Jade. "I don't hate women! It was just a...a thing I said! Our dragon shifter women can kick most of the men's asses! Which is why I would rather fight someone who fights like a man," he muttered at the end. "Less chance of losing."

Jade blinked, then giggled. Griff wondered if that worked for him, if people found it charming.

"Maybe I *am* slightly sensitive when it comes to such sayings," Jade said after a moment. "I've walked the streets in my kingdom as a woman, and the executions I had to line up after such an experience... Well, after that one time, I made sure to always present myself as royalty. Otherwise we might be hovering on the brink of extinction. Elven males *can* be very misogynistic. Ridiculous, isn't it?"

"I didn't know that," Griff said. "At least, I don't think I did. I thought all elves were sexually promiscuous and, um. Yeah." He didn't think adding 'vain and flighty' would be wise.

But Jade seemed to know what he'd held back. "Oh, we are, we are—if the elves are males. Or royalty. It's something I want to set about changing, which—" He sighed. "Well, that *is* why there's the little coup attempt, and the communing with nature."

"Shouldn't you be fighting for your kingdom?" Grlind asked, looking very much like he didn't approve of Jade at all.

Jade turned to him. "Orc, what do you think I am? Stupid? Of *course* I'm fighting for it, but there are more ways to win a war than to get hurt in it. Also, what good will it do my kingdom if I die? Then I won't be able to implement the changes I believe are necessary. Anyway, I've had enough of this tedious talk. Why are a dragon shifter, a fairy and an orc traveling together? It sounds like the start to a tasteless joke."

"You're a snob," Blaze observed.

Jade twirled a few strands of his black hair. "I prefer cultured, thank you very much."

Griff wasn't sure what to believe about the Storm King. He seemed too odd to pin down, so Griff stopped trying and just accepted the man for the time being.

"Well, I was attacked from beyond the veil," Griff began.

Jade's eyes widened. "You don't say!"

After Griff and Blaze had explained the entire tale, and Grlind had chimed in when it came to his part in it, Jade clapped his hands and beamed at them.

"Oh, an adventure! You *must* let me come. I have abilities that will help, and besides, any rending of the veil is a danger to all of us," Jade said. "It cannot be allowed. This is something that should have been shared at the World Magic Convention. Gods, talk about a waste. What started out as an annual meeting for world leaders has turned into a mockery and a cosplay event. Though the cosplay is actually very interesting. I saw *ten* of me last year! Of course none of them looked as good as me, but it was cute that they tried."

Griff laughed and shook his head. *Royalty. All of them are weird.*

But powerful, too, and that was part of the reason he had no objection to Jade joining their group.

And it'd be interesting to see if the spark between Grlind and Jade grew into a flame.

Chapter Twenty-Five

Traveling with an elf was a pain in the ass, no question about it. Blaze and Jade sniped back and forth more often than not.

Not even under duress would Blaze admit that the sniping was kind of fun, even if he sometimes got the feeling he wasn't catching on to an insult. He just called Jade a stuck-up dickhead and asked him how his kingdom was doing or something along those lines.

"Can I see the map again?" Griff asked, holding out his hand.

Grlind strode over and gave Griff the rolled map.

Griff opened it and frowned.

"What's wrong?" Blaze asked. That was definitely *not* a happy look.

Griff glanced up at the sky, to the suns, back at the map, then back at the suns before growling.

"That's a sexy as fuck sound," Blaze observed.

"Ick," Grlind commented. "No sexin' on an empty stomach."

"You just ate half an hour ago!" Jade exclaimed.

Grlind blushed a dark green. "Orcs need more food than most everyone else. We've a lot of muscle mass." He curled one arm, setting off a ripple of biceps, triceps and gods only knew what else–eps.

Griff was scowling at the map. He shook his head.

"What's wrong?" Blaze asked, trying to see what was causing Griff distress.

Griff growled again.

Blaze's cock twitched. Maybe they should take a break and —

"Something's off," Griff said. "Either Gia's mistaken in her cartography skills, or...or the world has changed? But it can't have changed. She must be wrong!"

Blaze looked around them. There were the Purple Mountains to the east, more dense forest to the west, behind them, to the north, the land looked the same as when they'd passed through as far as Blaze could tell, and ahead, to the south...well, all he could really see was more gods-be-damned forest.

"Er, what's missing on the map? Or here?" Blaze squinted at the map.

Griff thumped a spot on it. "We should be right here." He had his fingertip on a spot that had squiggles beneath it.

"Are those..." Blaze stopped. They were in a forest. He didn't think he was wrong about those squiggles not being trees.

"This is the Fauna and Fickle Forest." Griff tapped another part of the map. "We are in it now. We came through here —" He traced another path.

"Let me see that map," Jade demanded.

Griff ignored him. "We haven't veered off the path at all, have we?" He sounded so worried that Blaze knew he was afraid he'd forgotten that they *had* taken an alternate route.

Except, they hadn't. "Nope. We checked the map less than an hour ago and were on course."

"I'd like to see the map," Jade said again.

Griff didn't even glance at him. "So how are we in the forest, yet the map and the suns, the shadows they cast, all say we are here?" He tapped those squiggles again. "These are the Crosswise mountains, which are *beyond* the Purple Mountains. This makes no sense!"

"Can I *please* see the map?" Jade asked. Well, it was still closer to a demand, but the *please* had come out like it was painful to say.

Grlind snorted, but Griff must have heard Jade finally—or Jade had been close enough to polite to be acknowledged.

"Here." Griff turned to him and pointed at their spot on the map. "We are here, but we're not."

Jade held the map closer to his face. "Your sister must suck at cartography. This is clearly incorrect."

Grlind moved closer and looked over the top of Jade's head. "Oy, now, that's rude. Don't be an ass."

Jade tilted his head to one side. "I wonder how you'd like having your own personal hailstorm. Surely even an orc would get tired of being pelted after a few days."

Grlind grinned, which was more fearsome a look on him than not, but Jade couldn't see his expression. "Do your worst, Storm King." His amusement vanished, and he returned his attention to the map with a grunt. After a moment, he grunted again.

"What is the cause of that infernal sound you keep making?" Jade snapped. "You're breathing on the top of my head. You'll make my hair frizz."

Grlind exhaled slowly.

"How dare you — " Jade started.

Grlind talked over him. "This map has been altered somehow. It didn't look like this the last time we had it out, Griff."

"You were the one carrying it," Jade said.

Grlind glanced at him. "And what good would it do for me to alter it?"

"And what would he alter it with?" Blaze added, proud of himself for his contribution.

Jade frowned. "I don't know. Nothing else makes sense."

"There are other explanations," Griff said. "The map could be enchanted, bespelled — not by Gia. She wouldn't do that to me. Someone else, though."

Blaze looked at Grlind. "Are you sure the map changed?"

Grlind started to nod, then stopped. "Well, it had to. It's not like the land itself could change."

Jade's eyes widened as did Griff's.

Blaze had a very bad feeling about the whole situation. Very bad, indeed. "Then according to the map, which may or may not have changed on us, we're…standing on a mountain, but we're not. We're still in the forest, right?"

Griff nodded. "But it's possible the map was magicked by someone. It's impossible for the land itself to have moved."

Jade gave an exaggerated sigh. "If I call you a peasant, is that going to get me in trouble?"

"No," Griff snapped at the same time Blaze said, "Yes!"

Grlind just guffawed at all of them.

"Then I will refrain this time," Jade drawled. "However, it is *not* impossible to open the veil between the worlds. After all, *someone* put it into effect thousands of years ago. It was either that, or those who dwell on the other side would have murdered every Magical One in existence. Those others, the bland, magic-less ones, have always sought to destroy what they can't understand. And, alas." Jade gave another exaggerated sigh. "Not every Magical One managed to cross to our side before the veil was put in place."

Blaze gawped at him. "You're saying it could be someone with magic on the other side of the veil?"

Jade lowered his lashes, almost like he was being coy. "I'm saying it could be someone on either side of the veil, or even both sides of the veil. Perhaps there is more than one person involved. Perhaps there's a league, a...a *dark* league that seeks to reign through chaos and—"

"You're just making things up now," Grlind said.

"Aren't you?" Griff asked after a moment of utter silence.

Jade arched both thin eyebrows. "Am I?"

Chapter Twenty-Six

"I don't trust him. He's lying," Blaze muttered. "And he's an elf, so he could have done something to the map, or the trail, or...or this could all be an illusion."

Griff glanced furtively at Jade. "To what end, though?" He didn't know whether Blaze was right or wrong, but something was definitely off. "He needs to stop doing that annoying hand flap thing and answer questions."

"Where are Shadnay and Eleandross?" Blaze asked, stopping and catching hold of Griff's arm.

Griff looked around. "They were with us earlier..."

Blaze looked up at the foliage overhead. "When we were still on track?"

"When we looked at the map before, yes." Griff cocked his head and listened. The telltale lack of buzzing was disturbing. "I can't hear them. When did I last see them?" he wondered.

Blaze called out to Grlind, who was walking ahead of them. "Hey, Grlind!"

Grlind stopped and turned to him. "Yes?"

Jade kept walking, Griff noted.

"Have you seen the dragonflies since the map check?" Blaze asked.

Grlind opened his mouth and held one finger up. Then he frowned and closed his mouth. "Hm."

"What *is* the holdup?" Jade called back to them. "Are you all talking about me?"

"Don't flatter yourself," Griff retorted. Screw the man being royalty. He was annoying as a tick in the ass crack.

Jade sighed like he was the most put-upon man in the world. "You truly *are* a—"

Griff arched a brow at the elven king.

"Weird, wingless man," Jade finished.

Blaze growled and lunged toward the Storm King. Griff tackled him, almost taking Blaze to the ground. They stumbled while Grlind had words of some sort with Jade.

Blaze and Griff managed to keep from toppling over, but just barely. Griff pushed Blaze up against a nearby tree and sagged on him for support.

"Sorry," Griff said a moment later. "You don't want to attack the Storm King. He could kill you with the flick of a finger."

"He wouldn't," Blaze grumped. "Would he? Really?"

Griff shrugged halfheartedly. "I don't know, and that's the point. We don't know him. We might know *of* him, but that isn't the same thing. Don't you remember, he mentioned having men *executed!*"

Blaze gulped. "Do you think they were beheaded?"

"What does it matter how they died? They ended up dead, period," Griff retorted.

"There's still painful deaths and quick deaths, and any level in between," Blaze pointed out.

Griff closed his eyes and rested his head on Blaze's chest. "I don't know where Shadnay and Eleandross went, the world has warped somehow, either for real or as an illusion, we should have been at the place where my wings were lost—according to the map—hours ago and I think we're lost. Everything is a mess right now."

"Except for us," Blaze said. "You and me, together. We have each other. Everything else will come together as it should."

"You are…" Griff tipped his head back and looked up at Blaze. "Incredible. Sweet."

"Are you two done?" Jade asked. "We need to find a place to rest for the night."

Griff bit back a groan. "I just want to be with you, somewhere quiet and secluded."

"But you want to find your wings." Blaze cupped Griff's chin.

"Yes, of course, but we could be doing that, just you and me, and maybe the world wouldn't be off course," Griff couldn't help but say. He stepped back from Blaze. "Things are what they are, however. Maybe we can find somewhere to bed down for the night where you and I can have some privacy."

"That," Blaze drawled, "would be awesome."

Griff winked at him. "It would." And Griff had some very specific plans for what he would do with Blaze if they had enough time by themselves. "Let's go."

As soon as they started forward, Jade and Grlind started walking again, too.

"So no one has seen Shadnay and Eleandross for hours?" Griff asked loudly.

"No," Jade replied.

Grlind shook his head.

Griff frowned. Did that mean they were gone, off somewhere being happy dragonflies? Or had something bad happened to them?

He and Blaze discussed the options, and it was only when Jade pointed out a waterfall that Griff admitted to himself at least that perhaps they'd lost the dragonflies when the map or world changed.

It was a worrisome event—another worrisome event in a day full of them.

After they turned in for the night—without any privacy, so Griff had to settle for cuddling, which was good, too—Griff let his mind wander. He was in an almost trance-like state.

He saw himself floating – no, flying. He was flying, his wings so gorgeous and full, truly spectacular wings. He was flying, mostly content, a little distracted, then he was terrified, screaming, hurting. The pain as his wings were ripped from him was so intense he could almost feel it happen again.

Griff saw his wings flutter to the ground.

The ground! Griff studied it in his sleep state, taking in the details.

It looked nothing like the ground where he'd been told he was hurt.

Nothing like it at all.

Griff spent the rest of the night trying to decide if his memory was correct or not in its revelations. When the suns rose over the closest mountain, he still didn't have an answer on the subject.

Chapter Twenty-Seven

Blaze was up before anyone else. He slipped out from under Griff's arm and leg, then quietly made his way to the pack Grlind had set aside for the night.

Rather than risk making too much noise, Blaze hefted the whole bag up and glanced to make sure Grlind and Jade were still asleep. The two of them were a good half-dozen feet apart, and Jade wasn't facing Blaze, but he watched the Storm King's breathing for several moments until he was certain Jade wasn't feigning sleep.

Blaze returned to Griff's side and put one hand over Griff's mouth. Before he could nudge Griff awake, Griff's eyes shot open, and he grunted as he tried to sit up, hands going for Blaze's arm.

As soon as he saw that it was Blaze touching him, Griff slumped and leaned against Blaze.

"Come with me," Blaze said very quietly, then he stood and helped Griff to his feet.

The copse of trees they'd slept under was rife with twigs and other crunchy, noise-making things, so they had to pick their way very carefully until they were a good distance from the others.

"What's wrong?" Griff asked, his words hardly more than a wisp of breath.

Blaze moved them a little farther away, closer to the river running where, according to the map, it shouldn't be. He sat on a large rock there and patted it.

Griff came and sat beside him.

"Can you make some light?" Blaze asked. If he weren't such a fuckup himself, he could have done it. He hated not having any of his abilities anymore. His sister-in-law had damned well better give them back.

"Sure." Griff chanted just a few words, and a small glowing orb appeared in front of them. Though little, it cast a fair amount of light.

"Thanks." Blaze opened the pack. He found the map easily enough and took it out. Then he handed the bag to Griff. "Look in there and see if anything is in the bag that shouldn't be."

"Like what?" Griff took the pack. "And who would have put anything in there?"

Blaze shrugged. "We don't know Grlind, only the story he told us, and that elf is off. All the weird stuff has happened since he arrived. That could be a coincidence."

Griff nodded, but his eyes had a faraway look to them, as though he was lost in his thoughts. It didn't take long for those thoughts to spill out. "Or, Grlind could be taking advantage of Jade's appearance to frame him? If we're considering the theory that one —"

"Or both," Blaze interjected.

"Or both of our new acquaintances are sabotaging our quest, we have to reach out and consider as many possible scenarios as we can," Griff agreed.

Blaze scowled. "Um. Realistic ones, right?"

"Preferably, but with someone as powerful as the Storm King involved, there's no telling what's realistic and what isn't," Griff pointed out. "And if he's hiding because there's a coup, then it's even possible that Grlind has been searching for him for nefarious reasons, and our running into him has caused a delay in Grlind's plans."

Blaze's stomach dipped like it did when, as a dragon, he dove down toward the ground at breakneck speeds, only to pull up at the last second. Except he didn't get the adrenaline rush or fun that usually came with that experience.

"Or they could both be innocent," Griff continued.

"And someone else moved the world? Or the map?" Blaze asked. "But if they altered the map, they'd have had to know about the map. The only person besides me or you who knew of it was Gia."

"She didn't do it," Griff said flatly.

Blaze held up his hands. "I didn't say she did. I'm just stating the truth. You said we had to consider all possibilities. Maybe she told someone else after we left."

"Ugh!" Griff stood up. "She probably did. She'd at least have told Artaxis. He's her lover and king, after all."

"He's *your* king," Blaze felt compelled to point out. "But never been your lover?"

"Never. He's asked, but I'm not—he doesn't—there's just no—I didn't want—" Griff huffed and stomped one foot in an adorable display of temper.

Not that Blaze would tell him his fit was adorable. He had better self-preservation instincts than that.

"I wasn't interested," Griff finally got out. "I've always been a bit different than the rest of the fairies in my frolic."

"Are you sure you're *from* your frolic?" Blaze asked.

Griff gawped at him.

"What? I didn't mean it in a bad way. I was just asking. I mean, Bonny's not from our clan, and there are other dragon clans ours interacts with sexually and...well, okay. Mostly sexually." Blaze shrugged. "So I don't get why you're looking at me like I sprouted a third eyeball."

That at least got a snort of laughter from Griff. After which, he said, "I don't know, either. Shock, I guess, because Mom always said she couldn't begin to guess who my father was. She didn't even know which fairy from which frolic had impregnated her, according to Gia, and that's the norm for us. When a woman wants a baby, she's able to become pregnant. Mom was a true Love fairy, so, as I said, there's no telling who my father was, and in our frolic, it doesn't matter. There is no judgment, and there were plenty of males around to mentor me. There's a saying, it takes a frolic to raise a fairy."

"Huh." Blaze scratched his chin.

"Huh what?"

"It's just different from the dragon way. Not that I'm saying it's wrong or anything. It's interesting to learn about your ways. When you think about it, we don't really know much about each other," Blaze pointed out.

"This is true. We have time," Griff agreed. "I saw nothing odd in the bag, by the way. If it's charmed or magicked, I can't tell."

Blaze grumbled, mostly curse words. He'd wanted an easy solution to their problem. "Okay. Let's look at the map without them here."

Griff took one edge of the map and Blaze the other.

"We're here," Griff said after looking up at the sky. He touched a spot on the map. "Gods with goiters! That's not where it said we were when we stopped last night!"

Blaze blinked. "No, it isn't. Even if the map hadn't changed, the land is still wrong, though. Isn't it?"

Griff grimaced. "Yes. So maybe it's the map *and* the land that's been magicked?"

"It—"

"Wait!" Griff let go of the map and hopped up, suddenly more energetic than anyone should be in the early morning hours. "There was something… something I think I remembered, even thought I was sort of dreaming. It was…it was…" He trailed off and groaned. "Think, damn it!"

Blaze tucked the map away, then stood and rubbed Griff's shoulders. "Don't try so hard. And just because you were dreaming, sort of, doesn't mean you didn't remember the truth. Like your brain relaxes when you quit trying to think about so many things. Brilliant ideas come during sleep. Well, that's what I heard. I just have sexy dreams about all the ways I want you to fuck me."

Griff trembled and turned in Blaze's arms. "You dream of me fucking you?"

Blaze bobbed his head. "Oh yeah. All the time. Even when I'm awake."

Griff's nostrils flared, and he placed his hands on Blaze's hips. "There were still a few of the flowers in the bag."

Blaze's cock had started growing hard as soon as he'd mentioned what he dreamt about. He went hot then cold all over, then hot again. Lust hit him fast, scrambling his plan to talk about what was happening with the land and the map and the—well, everything.

He opened for Griff's kiss, moaning when Griff gripped him with more force and thrust his tongue in like he was staking a claim.

Blaze pushed frantically at Griff's clothing, seeking only to free his cock. As soon as he got his hands on that thick, rigid shaft, Blaze clenched his ass and shivered.

Gods, he'd turned into a horny bastard, more so than ever. He wanted Griff all the time.

And judging by the way Griff shoved at Blaze's trousers just enough to get them down past his cock and ass, it seemed that Griff was just as desperate for him.

Griff kept kissing him, teasing and dominating with his tongue, his teeth, his soft lips.

All Blaze could do was try to keep up. He had one hand on Griff's shaft, kind of stroking when he could get his brain to kick in and send the message to his arm and hand to move. With his other hand, he clutched at Griff's shoulder.

Then Griff did a bitey, tuggy thing to Blaze's lower lip that hurt just enough to send Blaze's arousal into a whole new level of urgent need.

Blaze made an embarrassingly mewl-like sound.

Griff spun him around. "Hands on the rock."

Blaze bent and slapped his palms against the boulder they'd been sitting on. He couldn't spread his legs much with his trousers still on.

Griff noticed and grumbled something, then Blaze was nude, and Griff was spreading his ass cheeks, rubbing slick, cool liquid over his hole.

Blaze really, *really* loved magic.

"You look so sexy like this," Griff praised as he slid one slick digit into Blaze's hole.

Blaze said, "Thank you." It wasn't his fault it came out missing all vowels. That was due to Griff finding his gland and giving it a nice, sweet rub.

"I should...should take my time, draw this out," Griff said, his voice stripped down to not much more than a series of rough grunts. "I'm a Love fairy."

And Blaze would love to get fucked, soon. He wiggled his hips and started shoving back, trying to get the message across since speech was beyond him.

Griff palmed his balls and the combination of fingering and fondling felt so good that Blaze's vision blurred. He gasped and panted and forgot about everything. All he could do was feel, and Griff kept pushing more and more *feeling* into him.

Blaze's dick was leaking pre-cum, his nerves pinging with electric shocks of pleasure. He lowered his chest down closer to the rock's surface and closed his eyes, chasing after a release that was tantalizingly close.

Then Griff's fingers were gone, and something thicker and hotter was pushing into Blaze's ass.

Blaze gulped, and his body seemed overloaded with pleasure. He felt raw and open in a way he couldn't comprehend. It had to do with more than just bodies meeting, mating. There was that bonding, the deeper ties forming and building, binding them and resonating between them.

Griff filled him with one long, slow thrust. He ran his hands up and down Blaze's flanks, over his back and shoulders.

He ground against Blaze's ass.

And just when he started to move, drawing his cock back until the fat cap stretched Blaze's ring, only then did Griff reach under Blaze and fist his shaft.

Blaze let the sounds fall from him — the needy, wanton, eager sounds he couldn't be embarrassed of giving to Griff.

Griff rasped with every thrust, saying Blaze's name, praising him, his body, his mind, his heart.

He pressed his chest to Blaze's back and rutted with short thrusts, as if he couldn't bear to pull out farther and put any distance between them. But he drove back in hard, those few inches he withdrew. His hips would barely separate from Blaze's ass before he was slamming them back against Blaze's butt.

He jacked Blaze steadily, and Blaze shoved a hand down to join him, needing to touch Griff as much as he could. Their hands together were perfect on his dick. Blaze didn't mind the scrape of rock against his skin, the bruises he'd have on his butt cheeks and hopefully other places from Griff holding on to him.

Nothing mattered but what they shared, the intimacy of it and the animalistic nature of fucking. The combination was deeper than anything Blaze had ever thought he'd experience.

His climax built and built until Blaze could hardly breathe. Then it hit, racing through him, sending his mind and body soaring as wave after wave of pleasure was pumped into him. He came so hard he lost track of everything until Griff snarled, the sound raw and wild and bare. He stiffened and rammed his cock in deep, his cum hot as it jetted into Blaze.

Blaze's legs gave out. He scraped his chest and forearm more as he went down.

If Griff hadn't had the agility to roll them, Blaze would have smacked his chin on the rock as well. Instead they landed on the ground, in a jumble of tangled limbs and sticky, sweaty masses.

Blaze might have dozed off. Eventually he became aware of his arm going numb and the suns beginning to rise. "Griff? We should get back to the others."

Groaning, Griff sat up and rubbed at one eye. "Yes, I guess so. We didn't do anything wrong, though. That's our bag, and our stuff in the bag."

"Right." Blaze knew that. He still felt like they'd stolen it. He sat up and winced. His ass was *sore*.

"Too rough?" Griff sounded so worried.

Blaze shook his head. "No. I like knowing I'll feel that—feel you, all day." *And possibly tomorrow. And the next day.* Blaze grinned. "It's like a dirty secret. Like I'm walking around with your dick still in me."

"Oh." Griff blushed. "That's good, then?"

"Very." Blaze wiped a smudge of dried lube off Griff's cheek. Gods only knew how it got there. Then he remembered— "Hey, the dream? What was it? The memory dream?"

Griff sighed, then said, "I remember! It was of when I was hurt. When I lost my wings. Only, the weird thing was, it wasn't in the spot I'd been told it happened in. And it made me wonder, the memory I had before of it, was that really a memory? Or was it something there because I'd been told it so many times?" Griff turned big, worried eyes on him. "Blaze, what if my king lied about where I was attacked?"

"Would he do that?" Blaze asked.

Griff didn't look happy at all. "I didn't think so. But what do I know? Artaxis could declare that I was injured on another planet, and everyone in the frolic would believe it. I just don't see why he'd do that, though."

Blaze was in a quandary. He didn't want to discount Griff's dream, which might be an actual memory, but he didn't want to alienate Griff from his frolic, either.

And he didn't know enough about Artaxis to make a call on his possible motives or whether or not he'd lie to Griff about the whole thing.

"Wait," Blaze said. "Didn't Gia know the truth?"

Griff glanced away. "I don't know anymore. I don't know if she knew what I was doing, or if Artaxis *told* her what I was doing afterward. After I'd been hurt. All I have to go on is what I've been told, and I don't know if my memories of any of it are even my own now."

Chapter Twenty-Eight

Try as he might, Griff couldn't discern whether or not Grlind and/or Jade was lying to them in any context. The Storm King was a pain in the ass, but in Griff's experience, royalty always had a sense of entitlement that made them obnoxious at times.

With the exception of Blaze, who was, after all, the second son of a king and queen, brother to the current king in his clan.

Even Artaxis had his moments where he went full-out raving diva on people. Griff had never experienced one of his king's tantrums firsthand, nor had any of them aimed at him. He'd seen Artaxis lose it a handful of times, though, and while most of those events had been justified, a couple had been more those of a spoiled child not getting his or her way.

Griff groaned and rolled his neck, chasing off a mild pain there. He had to question every memory he had, and it made believing in himself very difficult. That reflected in what he thought he knew about almost everything, and who he was, even.

Blaze sighed and nuzzled the back of Griff's neck. "Got a kink? Well, besides the obvious one for being bossy when it comes to sex. Which I like. A lot."

"Hah. Yes, it's a bit tight back there." He rolled his eyes, knowing he'd just left Blaze an opening.

"I bet it is," Blaze leered — Griff could hear it in his voice. "*Real* tight." He tickled the top of Griff's crack.

Griff tried not to laugh to no avail. He ended up squealing and scrambling to his feet. "Behave," he said when he saw Blaze's intention in his eyes. "We've got to get back to the others. If you're a good boy, I might just bind your hands tonight and..." He smirked as Blaze whimpered. *Let him think about what I might do after I have his wrists bound together. He'll anticipate it all day.*

Griff would damn sure have to live up to those expectations, too.

Once he had them both clothed properly again, Griff hefted the bag over one shoulder. "I think I'll spend some time talking to the Storm King today. See if I can get a good reading on him. Who knows, maybe he'll admit to messing with us all just for a whim. Elves can be flighty."

Griff immediately felt bad for the comment. "Then again, the same has been said of most fairies. Especially the Love fairies. We're only good for fucking."

Blaze surprised him by stopping Griff, catching a hold of him by one arm. "No."

"No?" Griff repeated. "No what?"

"No, you aren't only good for fucking," Blaze explained slowly.

"I didn't think I was," Griff assured him. And for the most part, that was probably true.

Before they reached the area they'd bedded down in, they heard a ruckus coming from that direction.

Blaze stilled Griff once again, tensing noticeably. They exchanged worried looks. Griff tried to make out what the sounds could be. His first were sexual thoughts—bodies slapping rhythmically, grunts of pleasure and exertion.

Which made him grimace as he wondered if Grlind and Jade were doing the deed.

Except a low curse sounded, followed by a muffled voice, one that definitely carried a strained, frantic tone.

Blaze held up one finger and stared at Griff.

Griff stared right back. If the dragon thought he'd just hang back and let Blaze go barging into whatever was happening, he had another think coming.

Griff inhaled, and caught it then, a whiff of something metallic on the breeze. The breeze—which was blowing from the direction of their little encampment.

The grunts and thuds didn't sound sexual at all, Griff realized. He gripped Blaze's hand tightly. They exchanged a look, each trying to read the other.

Griff shivered when a low moan reached them. *That isn't a sound of pleasure.*

Blaze tipped his chin at Griff, as if he knew of and agreed with Griff's deduction.

Blaze looked back toward their encampment. He scowled, clearly wavering over what to do.

But Griff knew only one thing. If Grlind and Jade, or even one of the two, were innocent of the hijinks happening around them, then he couldn't stand back and leave them to battle whoever, or whatever, was in the camp now.

Because something most definitely was, and it was either friend or foe, just as Jade and Grlind were.

Knowing who was who or what, those answers eluded Griff. But he couldn't stand back and do nothing.

He tugged on Blaze's hand. Griff raised his other hand, bringing his thumb and forefinger together until they almost touched.

Blaze shook his head.

Well, Griff understood that—if they were small, they'd be easily defeated.

He also understood something else. If whoever was attacking wanted to hurt him and Blaze, they might not be looking for them in minimized form. Altering their size might allow him and Blaze to use the element of surprise.

The scuffling was still going on. Griff gestured for Blaze to come closer. Once he did, Griff explained his plan.

Blaze gave him a quick kiss, then nodded.

They needed to see who was doing what and decide from there whether or not to intervene. It was strange that there might be fighting occurring and yet there were no truly loud noises coming from it.

Magic. But whose? Griff wouldn't know until they could get closer, which meant he needed to do a little magic of his own.

He just hoped it didn't get them both stepped on.

Chapter Twenty-Nine

Blaze's heart stopped the second he spotted the fiends attacking Grlind and Jade. He supposed it shouldn't have been such a shock—elves and fiends were mortal enemies. So were orcs and fiends, dragons and fiends...everyone and fiends, except for other fiends, of course.

Fiends never turned on each other.

And they were viciously difficult to defeat.

Griff clenched Blaze's hand and fear etched his features. His eyes were huge as he looked from the battle to Blaze.

Fiends called for a retreat and some kind of plan.

Blaze tugged Griff back a good distance, keeping track of the fiends in case some of the bastards spotted them. Not likely, maybe, but possible.

As soon as he had Griff far enough away, Blaze pulled him close and whispered in his ear. "A half-dozen fiends, Griff. We aren't armed enough to take them on. Even the Storm King is going to lose to them."

"Fiends." Griff shuddered. "I couldn't remember the name of them. They're so…" He shuddered again.

"Scary," Blaze finished for him. It was true. Just seeing a fiend could strike fear in the heart of someone and freeze them on the spot.

Which might have been why fiends were rarely defeated. There were disagreements about what fiends truly looked like, but Blaze knew the truth of their appearance.

They were supernatural beings that drew from viewers' fears. Whatever gave someone nightmares, whatever terrified them asleep or awake, *that* was what each fiend appeared to be to them.

Sometimes even the viewer didn't understand what they were seeing. Not everyone's fears were coalesced into an easily understood nightmare.

Blaze wasn't sure what he'd seen. He refused to dwell on it.

"If we have to fight them, I don't know if I can," Blaze admitted. "What if I look at them and see you?"

"See me? Why—" Griff frowned, then beamed at him. "Oh! I remember what they are! Well, I don't know what they're really called. We were told tales of frighteners when we were children. That's what they are. They steal into your mind and display your fears. Why would you see me? You're not afraid of me, Blaze."

There was no way he'd explain that all of his worst fears had to do with something bad happening to Griff. "What did you see?" Blaze asked.

Griff shrugged. "Nothing scary. I don't think, after what I went through, that they could scare me more."

Blaze felt his eyebrow winging up his forehead without him even having to think about it. "Hey! If you don't have any fears…"

"Then they can't be used against us," Griff said. "I mean, I'm afraid of never finding my wings again, but how would they make that into a...a...a thing?" He shrugged. "Do they have magic? Besides that?"

Blaze nodded. "Yeah, but I don't know what kind of magic other than the *scare the shitballs out of you* kind."

"Shitballs?" Griff glanced back over his shoulders. "We need to help Grlind and Jade. Even if they might not be on our side."

"I wonder if the fiends just stumbled on them or if someone sent them," Blaze murmured.

"Are they for hire?" Griff asked.

Blaze had no idea. "I don't know." He hated being so stupid. Maybe he wasn't dumb about everything, like he knew...well, he knew some things. Just not the stuff he wished he knew.

"Whatever you're thinking must be unpleasant," Griff observed. "Do you have any idea how to fight the fiends?"

As much as Blaze wanted to be Griff's hero, he couldn't lie. "No. I've never fought them and have only heard about other dragons who've fought—and lost—against the fiends."

"Don't they burn?"

"I don't have fire, so it doesn't matter," Blaze mumbled. "And if I freak out because I'm terrified..."

"We can fix that."

"How?" Blaze asked just as Griff tore a strip off his tunic. "Ohhhhh."

"Ohhhhh." Griff smiled briefly before he placed the material over Blaze's eyes.

Blaze huffed as darkness encompassed him. "Griff? I can't see to fight."

"Uh—" Griff stopped tying a knot behind Blaze's head. "Your other senses can't lead you? Scent and sound? I thought dragons had really sharp senses."

"Not sure they'd work against fiends. Fear could appear in different ways, right?"

Griff removed the material. "Damn it, yes. It could manifest in a scent or sound, certainly. Why didn't I think of that?"

"Maybe I'm rubbing off on you," Blaze said.

Griff pointed at him. "Don't. Don't you start insulting yourself."

Blaze ducked his head, embarrassment warming his cheeks. "What are we going to do?" he asked softly.

"We're going to go fight. We're not going to let fear have any sway over us. We can't." Griff tucked a finger under Blaze's chin. "If we lose, if I die—"

Blaze couldn't have stopped the growl if his life had depended on it. He yanked Griff to him and said, "You won't die. *Ever!*" and before Griff could even blink, Blaze crushed his mouth to Griff's, tasting him, feeding him that determination not to even consider dying.

Just as suddenly as he'd grabbed Griff, Blaze set him back a half step. If he didn't, there'd be sex, and sex while Grlind and Jade were being attacked wasn't cool at all.

"We won't lose," he told Griff. He might have trouble believing it himself, but he'd damn well make it happen. They'd be the first to defeat the fiends.

"No, we won't. But we must be bigger, and you need a weapon." Griff chanted, and a moment later, both he and Blaze were no longer small, and a long, deadly-looking sword had appeared in front of Blaze. The hilt was plain, nothing fancy at all, but the length of the sword was covered in etched symbols or words. Blaze didn't know which.

Griff's breath hitched, and he drew his hands away from the weapon. "Gods, it's the Sword of Synchrony. It doesn't just take lives, it destroys their soul, utterly! They are *dead* dead!"

Blaze yanked his own hands back. "I don't want to touch it!" Souls were sacred, and they were definitely vital to reincarnation. If one was destroyed, that was the end of a person's life. They were just...*gone*.

"It's what the goddess Ahndwa saw fit to send you," Griff said. "I wouldn't risk insulting Her."

Insulting the goddess of war was unthinkable. Blaze bit his bottom lip. "Thank you, Ahndwa. Please guide my hands."

"No one has seen it in centuries," Griff said reverently as Blaze grasped the hilt.

Blaze felt a current unlike any he'd ever experienced. It zapped from the sword to his palm and fingers, up his forearm to his biceps, triceps, shoulder and down to his chest. It hit his heart with a painful jolt that made his ears ring with a shout he never loosed. The metal warmed in his hand and seemed to throb. A swell of power thrummed throughout his body.

"Blaze." Griff placed a hand over his own heart. "You...your eyes. All of you..."

Blaze didn't get to hear the rest of what Griff was saying. A fiend appeared behind Griff, as if transported there.

Blaze roared as the creature doubled in size and raised razor-sharp talons over Griff's head. Blood dripped from them as Griff spun around.

Griff neither screamed nor shrank back. He raised one hand and sent a bright ball of green and gold flames at the fiend.

The flames hit the creature, and the fiend shrieked, stumbling back.

Blaze moved with a speed he had never before possessed. The sword hummed. He felt it, heard it, and his heartbeat aligned with that song.

It empowered him, and he surged past Griff. The sword's musical sound grew louder as it sliced through the air.

Those green and gold flames had done some damage to the fiend, but nothing like the sword slicing through flesh and bone. Blaze had never held such a mighty weapon, one so finely made that it could cut through a living being like it was nothing of substance at all.

He was equal parts horrified and intrigued as he watched Synchrony cut the fiend in half. Some small part of his brain was reminded that, for all Blaze knew of the creatures, they could be boneless, hence the ease of doing what he'd just done.

Except he saw white bones before the blood and entrails went everywhere.

"Oh…oh gods!" Griff spun around and retched.

Blaze wanted to reach for him and comfort Griff, but the sword was a living thing in his grasp, and it was mightier than he was.

There was no releasing the beast he'd been handed. His fingers wouldn't obey his mind's command to do so.

Blaze was jerked a foot forward. "Griff! Griff!"

Griff wiped at his chin and mouth. "Mmph."

"*GRIFF!*" Blaze shrieked because he was being pulled away from his bonded. "The sword is—ow!"

"About to dislocate your shoulder." Griff ran over to him. "Let it lead. It won't stop until its task is complete."

Blaze could barely keep up with it. He wasn't even certain his feet were touching the ground.

Griff ran behind him. "I'm sorry! I didn't know!"

Blaze got it. Griff hadn't known he'd end up being attached to the bossiest sword in all of existence.

But it was a good thing he was, because the moment the rest of the fiends came into view, Blaze's mind recoiled in horror. His fears were, apparently, numerous after all. He saw Griff dead, dying, in agony. There was Fyre being eviscerated and his parents in various stages of decay.

Blaze saw it all in the blink of an eye, then his arm was swinging, his feet moving in a skillful dance he shouldn't have known.

He saw Grlind, bleeding and down, heard Jade screaming, but what was real and what was a nightmare, he couldn't say. When he sliced through one Fyre lookalike, it almost killed Blaze.

Then there was Griff, on his knees, begging for his life.

"Blaze!" Griff shouted. "Kill it!"

That voice came from behind Blaze. Whether he'd have listened to it if he'd had the choice, Blaze would never know, because the sword called, and it took. There was nothing he could do but watch in complete horror as Synchrony speared the kneeling Griff right through the heart.

Blaze screamed. He was going to lose his mind! He couldn't—

"I'm here!" Griff grabbed him, all but climbing onto Blaze. "I'm right here. I'm always going to be here, with you. See? The sword isn't trying to get me."

Blaze gasped and gasped until his world stopped spinning and the insane chaos in his head slowed down. "Griff?"

Griff was in front of him, holding him, arms wrapped around Blaze's middle. "Right here. I'll hang on. We'll fight together."

"It was you," Blaze got out as his arm was jerked up and outward again. "Gods, they're all you!" Every one of the fiends had morphed into a matching version of Griff.

Jade bellowed and leapt on one of them. Grlind shot up from the ground, a gash in his chest, but undeterred as he tackled another fiend. Blaze was faced with two.

"Close your eyes," Griff whispered. "Now you have the sword to guide you, and me, right here."

Blaze tried to close his eyes, but he saw the sword driving through the body of the fiend that had taken on Griff's appearance. He might never be able to close his eyes again.

Griff unwound from him and leapt toward the sword.

Blaze shouted, but Griff only grabbed the hilt, his hand covering Blaze's as much as possible.

"I'm right here," Griff said. "We're together." Tiny lines appeared around the outer edges of his eyes and framed the corners of his mouth. "Now!"

Pain burned down Blaze's hand and arm, following the path the power had taken moments earlier.

Something was wrong, something was off, but he didn't have time to figure out what. The sword was leading him—and Griff—and the battle raged on.

There would be no losing to the fiends this time. Blaze knew it as surely as he knew his soul was now forever darkened.

Chapter Thirty

Two things occurred to Griff as he clung to Blaze. The first was that he hadn't known he could call on a goddess. He couldn't have named the deities had his life depended on it before that moment when he'd reached for Ahndwa's help.

Second, the Sword of Synchrony was possessing Blaze, at least to a degree.

And he realized a third thing as Blaze destroyed the last fiend. There was more locked away in his mind than an average Love fairy should be aware of.

Blaze's gasp brought Griff's focus back to his bonded. Blaze's eyes were still glowing with an eerie glint of silver in their amber depths. His face was flushed, and his features slightly altered, as if blurred. It took Griff a moment to realize he was seeing flickering, shadow images flitting over Blaze's features. It was eerie and terrifying.

"Blaze?"

Blaze gasped again. He reached for Griff's cheek, his mouth moving and with a lost look as he trembled.

"Blaze!" Griff didn't know why he was so scared, didn't know what was happening to his bonded.

Then Blaze threw his head back and screamed.

Griff stumbled back, propelled by a supernatural force that burned when it slapped at him. Blaze's entire body convulsed, and an orange-gold glow encompassed him.

He levitated off the ground just as the colors around him grew brighter.

Griff shouted his name again. The light was too much — he squinted and shielded his eyes. Heat rolled off Blaze in waves.

With his retinas close to being singed, Griff had only a second to see the flames shoot from Blaze's appendages, from his mouth and eyes. Griff felt the pain of it, his insides burning torturously as Blaze screamed.

Then as suddenly as the agony had begun, it ceased. Griff collapsed, though he'd no sooner hit the ground than he began crawling, forcing his eyes open, searching for his bonded.

When he saw Blaze, Griff's heart almost stopped. Blaze was on bended knee, head down, puffs of smoke leaving his nostrils with every exhalation. Ahndwa stood before him, one hand in Blaze's hair, the other holding the Sword of Synchrony.

Griff didn't dare interfere with the goddess. He managed to crawl to Ahndwa's side where he knelt, head bowed in a show of respect.

When Ahndwa touched his head, Griff whimpered in a mix of fear and gratitude. The goddess' touch could be a blessing or a curse.

She stroked her fingers over his scalp, then moved them down to his face, her touch leaving a heated trail behind. When she reached his chin, Ahndwa pressed up, and Griff raised his head just enough to look at her knees.

Another push, and he dared look higher. When he gazed past her smiling lips, past her strong nose and to her dark green eyes, Griff felt a pressure in his head, like someone had stuffed it too full and it was close to bursting.

He winced and would have reached for his temples but was unable to move.

The goddess stared at him, and he felt exposed, vulnerable and elated at the same time.

"What have they done to you, my *brioghi*?" Ahndwa asked with such tenderness that Griff's eyes welled.

He couldn't answer. His mind was still a chaotic disaster. Yet with each sweep of her fingers over his skin, Griff's panic and fear ebbed, to be replaced with a peace that was pure and comforting. There was no need for him to feel anything other than what the goddess gave him. Griff accepted it, sinking into the gift of her touch.

She murmured words he didn't understand, and Griff's eyelids grew heavy, too heavy to hold open. The sensations he felt altered. A new energy flowed into him, a familiar, loving one. Blaze's presence was mingled with his, and Griff's with Blaze's. It was another gift from their goddess, a blessing, and that was all he knew of it.

Then slowly, the feeling of safety and comfort waned, though it didn't leave him altogether. The connection with Blaze was still there, too, yet not as strong as it had been.

It was still a treasure, a bond unlike any Griff had ever heard of. He slowly opened his eyes and found that Blaze was still kneeling. The goddess was fading out, her smile still fond, her touch still on them. The Sword of Synchrony was strapped to her back.

Griff was relieved she hadn't left it with Blaze. The sword was a blessing and a curse.

Ahndwa grew dimmer, then was gone as a breeze wafted over them. Blaze raised his head, his gaze seeking out Griff's immediately.

Blaze reached for him, and Griff moved into his arms.

Behind him, Griff heard someone clearing their throat.

He ignored them in favor of holding on to his bonded. Blaze held on to him with equal strength and need.

"You do realize that a goddess never blesses without there being a cost."

Griff squinched his eyes shut upon hearing Jade's words. He had no doubt Ahndwa had blessed him and Blaze.

"She freed my fire," Blaze rasped. "She freed my dragon. She brought us closer together."

A small, angry part of Griff wanted to know why she hadn't given *him* his wings back—or his memory. He snuffed that part of himself down. All that mattered was that Blaze had recovered that which had been taken from him.

"I'll pay whatever the cost for that," Griff murmured to Blaze. He wasn't taunting Ahndwa.

"There'll be a cost," Jade said. "There always is."

Blaze hugged Griff tighter, then loosened his hold and leaned back. Griff opened his eyes and saw that Blaze was looking beyond him.

"Where's Grlind?" Blaze asked.

"Here." Grlind sounded pained.

Griff wiggled and, in short order, stood along with Blaze. Grlind was sitting with his back against a tree. Blood had pooled beside him.

"Healed," Grlind added. "For the most part."

"Is that through your own power?" Griff asked.

Grlind cast a look at the Storm King. "No."

Before Griff could ask what he meant, Jade huffed and took one step, only to whimper and collapse.

"Shit!" Grlind scrambled toward the fallen elf.

Griff and Blaze reached him first. Griff smelled blood. "He's hurt!"

He shoved at Jade's robes and found them heavy with blood. The dark red and black material had hidden it well.

Griff grabbed the ripped fabric and tore. "Gods!" Three deep gashes marred Jade's side.

"Is he hurt anywhere else?" Blaze asked.

"Let me see!" Grlind demanded.

They stripped Jade quickly and found another deep wound on his left thigh.

"And he used his gods-be-damned powers to heal me?" Grlind growled. "Foolish king!"

Griff shook his head. He didn't understand any of it—Ahndwa coming to his and Blaze's aid, the sword, the release of Blaze's abilities, blessings and debts and healings—and he couldn't concentrate on any of it. Friend or foe, or something in between, the Storm King needed their help.

If he died, the chaos wouldn't be confined to the elven world.

Chapter Thirty-One

Even as Blaze tried to help Griff and Grlind treat the Storm King, he was aware that something was different inside him. Killing the fiends with the Sword of Synchrony had affected him all the way to his soul.

Every time he'd killed with it, he'd felt the sword grow warm and heard it sing just as it did when slicing through the air. He'd felt the lives leaving the bodies, felt the fear and pain and that final moment when life had blinked out.

And those souls were utterly destroyed. There'd be no coming back for them. He'd have to carry that knowledge, the guilt of his responsibility in the fiends' deaths, with him forever.

Just as he'd be at the goddess Ahndwa's beck and call. That was the price he'd paid to defend his bonded. Jade had been right when he'd said the goddess didn't bless freely. Blaze would be her champion in the living realm. He had a feeling Griff wouldn't be happy about that at all.

And he also believed Ahndwa would require payment from Griff, but in what manner, Blaze had no idea. He and Griff needed to talk, alone, once they had the chance.

With Jade growing ever paler and having long since ceased speaking, Blaze worried the elf wouldn't make it. He didn't know much about the elven world politics, but they were probably just as screwed up as the dragons' were, if not more so.

Everything was becoming more complicated, and Blaze wasn't smart enough to figure out how to fix any of it. He wanted to bang his head against the nearest tree, he was so frustrated with himself.

Then there was that creepy word Ahndwa had called Griff—*brioghi*. What did that even mean? The way Ahndwa had caressed Griff's hair, too, had been…almost possessive or fond or…

"Argh!" Blaze closed his eyes and tried to get his emotions under control. He was in such a weird state and had never experienced anything like it before.

He couldn't hide behind his eyelids, however. Grlind had sent him to find some staggo weeds. They weren't far from the encampment. The black-stalked plants had thick veins running through them. Those veins pulsed rhythmically as the blue-petals of the flower swayed back and forth.

They were fucking weird plants. "Weeds," Blaze muttered. "They're just weeds."

He knelt and swooped up a handful of them.

And shrieked when each plant emitted a keening sound. "Oh my fucking gods!" Blaze yelped, dropping the plants. "Fuck! Fuck!"

He heard the thud of footsteps and spun around to see Grlind barreling toward him.

"What the *fuck*!" Blaze shouted at him.

Grlind slowed down and almost smiled. "Oh, aye. The weeds are also known as banshee blooms. That's a horrible sound they make."

Blaze glared at him. "I killed them!"

Grlind cocked his head and scratched his rounded chin. "Were you gonna kill them any less if they didn't make noise? Because you *were* gonna fetch them for me. We need them for Jade."

Blaze looked from Grlind to the weeds. "It's different when they scream."

"Still kills the plants just as much as when they don't." Grlind stalked past him and picked the plants up. "A few more should do it."

Blaze slapped his hands over his ears but still heard the gods-awful racket as the weeds were snapped off.

Then Grlind nudged him, and they hurried back to Jade and Griff.

Jade's breathing was labored, but the bleeding had ceased.

Grlind looked grim as he began mashing the staggo between his palms. In short order, he had a thick, disgusting looking paste that he applied to the Storm King's wounds.

Thunder clapped overhead, and the skies turned dark.

"Must hurt," Grlind observed. "I'm sorry, Jade, but I've got nothing else to use. It's this or death."

Jade shuddered just as lightning split a tree in half, way too close for Blaze's comfort.

After another bolt hit, Jade opened his eyes just enough to see a hint of the irises. "I might...prefer...death," he panted out.

Grlind clucked his tongue. "Now, now. Don't be a brat, Storm King." Then Grlind took Jade's hands in his. "Take back some of what you gave me," he urged. "I can recover from you using a bit of my life force."

Jade started to shake his head, but Grlind leaned over and growled at him. "You're the king of your people. Do what you must do to help them. You dying won't help them, will it?" He leaned even closer. "Just enough to keep yourself alive and give the staggo time to work. That's all you have to take from me. It'll mean a day off my lifespan, at most, and if you die, I'll kill myself just to spite you."

"You wouldn't," Jade gasped, eyes finally opening wide. "No!"

It'd be the height of insult, Blaze assumed.

Jade stared for a moment, then he began chanting softly. Despite that tone, the power of the chant was evident in the way the storm suddenly burst free, rain and hail pounding down around them.

None of it touched them. The wind swirled, sending the leaves and dirt into a panicked dance, a tornadic melody of nature's madness—or the Storm King's anger.

It lasted less than a minute, then there was complete silence and eerie stillness.

Until they all had to breathe.

Grlind sat back on his haunches as Jade sprung up into a sitting position. At the same time, he threw a hard punch that caught Grlind right on the jaw.

Despite his size, Grlind went flying backward and landed with a thud.

"What in the world is wrong with you?" Griff snapped at Jade.

Jade was shaking as he pointed at Grlind. "That...that *fool* didn't give me a day! He pushed *years* into me. *Years!* Do you know what that means?"

Blaze noted that the wounds were only very fine, very faded scars now.

Jade didn't wait for an answer. "It means he could drop dead at any time! A day is a day, but years? *Years!*"

The Storm King wasn't the selfish bastard Blaze had thought him to be. Jade was clearly, honestly distraught over Grlind's sacrifice.

"Well, trying to knock his head off could sure shorten Grlind's life span," Blaze pointed out. "I'd bet a thank-you would have been the appropriate response."

"And you are healed up completely," Grlind said, rubbing his jaw. "I didn't mean to give so much, but what's done is done, and what have I got to do in my life other than this quest? Nothing. There is no place in this world for a solitary orc."

He didn't sound sad or as if he wanted pity. Instead, Grlind spoke as if what he said were merely a fact.

Jade began to argue with Grlind. Blaze blocked them out as he focused on Griff. "What did the goddess demand from you?"

Griff frowned at him. "Demand? Nothing. I don't think she did. I mean, I could have forgotten, but I don't think that's the case. She touched me and it felt...felt good, like a mother's touch. And she called me *brioghi*, which I've never heard before."

"*Brioghi?*" Jade asked, standing as he held up a hand toward Grlind. "Wait, orc. Griff, who called you *brioghi?*"

Griff shivered. "What does it mean?"

Jade walked over to Griff, a troubled look on his face. "Who called you *brioghi?*"

Griff bit his bottom lip and shook his head. Then he finally answered. "Ahndwa."

Jade took a step back. "Who are you really, Griff? Stop lying to us and tell us."

Blaze spun to face Jade. "Don't call him a liar. Storm King or not, I will kick your ass!"

Grlind moved to stand behind Jade. "Why would you ask such a thing, Jade?"

Jade raised those damned kingly eyebrows of his and said, "Because Ahndwa called him her son."

Chapter Thirty-Two

Griff stumbled back. "Son? No, you must be wrong, or...or she meant it in that non-familial way. And we're *all* her sons and daughters anyway! She's a goddess and —"

Blaze was staring at him, mouth open. Jade had his head cocked to the side — those damned imperious eyebrows arched. Grlind merely watched him.

"What?" Griff demanded.

"You..." Blaze gulped and glanced at the others, then back at him. "You kinda look like her?"

Griff shook his head, in full-blown denial. "No! I don't!" He had parents, real fairy parents...somewhere. "Gia's my sister! I remember her! We grew up together."

Jade tutted. "Dear fairy, that doesn't mean shit. She could be your sister in fact or in name only if you're a foundling."

"I'm not a foundling!" Griff shouted, angry and scared and ready to hit someone. "Stop it! Stop lying to me!" His head throbbed, and he dropped to his knees, cradling it with his hands.

"Griff!" Blaze was right there, wrapping him in strong arms. "Shut up, Jade, and get away from us!"

"I'm only trying to help," Jade said in something close to a whine. "I wasn't being deliberately cruel."

Griff ignored Jade, ignored Grlind. He didn't pay much attention to Blaze, either, because the pounding in his head was excruciatingly painful.

The fear threatening to smother him was even worse.

"Can't think, can't think," he muttered between gasped breaths. Nothing would slow down in his head. He had flashes of memories and snippets of conversations that he was trying really hard not to doubt. What was real, and what wasn't? He'd asked himself that for a long time now. "I don't know."

"Get the fuck away from us, asshole," Blaze snapped.

"I didn't mean to upset him," Jade said. "I —"

Blaze roared, and his skin heated up to an almost uncomfortable temperature. Griff opened his eyes just in time to see streams of flames shoot from Blaze's mouth.

Jade scrambled back, eyes huge, and Griff felt it.

Blaze's body shook and grew hotter. His skin rippled and thickened, and his bones popped and shifted.

From one second to the next, Blaze transformed. Griff was no longer held in a man's arms, but instead had a huge, powerful beast wrapped around him, sheltering him from the world.

It stopped the spinning in his head. How could he freak out when Blaze was suddenly this glorious, gorgeous dragon?

Griff twisted around to see more of him. Blaze was a vibrantly colored dragon, his scales shades of red, orange, yellow and gold. His paws were tipped with long, sharp black talons, and his wings — they were stunning, with thick tendons and bones covered in those bright colors.

He had ridges along his spine, and a long, sharp-tipped tail that he was twitching, thumping it from side to side on the ground. Griff returned his attention to Blaze's head. The triangular head and broad jaw set off the foot-long canines that were exposed when Blaze gnashed his teeth.

He had a thin, bisected tongue that was a deep red, and his eyes were still the same color, only much larger as he looked at Jade and snarled again.

"You're beautiful," Griff murmured, reaching up to touch one small, pointed ear. "Gods, Blaze. You are truly amazing."

Blaze cut off mid-bellow and swung his head around to press the tip of his nose to Griff's.

Griff giggled, the soft warm puffs of Blaze's breath tickling his neck. He stroked Blaze's face and was surprised at how smooth the scales were. "I would have thought they'd be rough, hard."

Blaze puffed and sent Griff's hair fluttering. Then he licked Griff, and Griff started imagining things he probably shouldn't have, all things considered. Blaze grunted and nudged Griff closer to him, tucking him in and curling up around him again.

Griff pressed closer, and Blaze stopped grumping at Jade.

"Gods and demons, he might just be able to beat an orc in a fight," Grlind said. "I've never seen an actual dragon before. Just heard stories about them."

Blaze rumbled.

Griff closed his eyes again and felt himself grow even calmer. He must have dozed off, because the next thing he knew, he was opening his eyes and the sun was higher than it had been. The air carried the scent of stewed meat on it, and his stomach growled almost as loud as Blaze had done.

Griff murmured and rubbed his cheek against Blaze's side. "Time for lunch?" They'd wasted too much of the day, but he couldn't regret it.

"Food's done, then we should get moving after we eat," Grlind called out. "No sense in staying where the fiends have found us once already."

Griff woke up fully and patted Blaze. "We need to eat, then get out of here. It's not safe."

Blaze raised his head, then got to his feet. He nudged Griff back before shaking from head to tail. He shifted forms and stretched. "Ah, gods, that felt wonderful!"

"I'm glad," Griff said, admiring Blaze's nude form.

Blaze winked at him, then pulled him into a hug. "Whatever happens, I'll be here with you. If you fall apart, I'll pick you up and put you back together. But maybe…maybe you shouldn't fight it when your mind is pulling up memories."

Griff clung to him. "But I don't know what's real and what isn't! What if everything I've known is a lie? What if my memories aren't my own, but ones told to me? What if—" He couldn't go on.

"No matter what, which ifs happen and which don't, you are *not* alone, Griff." Blaze leaned his head back and stared into Griff's eyes. "Whether you're the son of a goddess or a full-blooded fairy, you are still the exact same person you were before Ahndwa said anything. You're still the same man I love."

Griff's eyes teared up, and he pressed a kiss to Blaze's lips. The taste of Blaze was arousing, though the hint of smoke on his lips was new.

When he pulled back, Griff cupped Blaze's cheek. "You are a very smart man, Blaze. Wise in ways few people are."

Blaze snorted. "Uh-huh."

Griff narrowed his eyes at him.

"I'm not calling you a liar," Blaze said quickly. "I just—well, I know I'm not smart like most people are."

"You're smarter," Griff stated firmly. "And I'm not going to hear you claim otherwise. You know what truly matters, and you have a heart as big as the dragon you shift into."

Blaze blushed, and a pleased smile curved his lips. "Thank you."

Griff smiled back at him. At least he'd done something right finally, instead of just losing his wits and having a meltdown.

Chapter Thirty-Three

Blaze couldn't help but notice the speculative looks Grlind and Jade kept giving him throughout the day. It made him puff up a bit, stoked his pride and ego. They weren't sure about him, and he'd impressed them with his shift. Maybe even scared them a little, which wasn't something to be proud of...yet he was. They both had powers—Grlind, his great strength and wit, Jade, the power to tear up the world with storms, and his elven magic. It was nice to be able to compete with them, or at least not feel as if he were a loser.

But he tried not to gloat or anything like that. Before he'd met Griff, he would have strutted like he was the cock of the walk. He'd learned a little humility since then.

Plus, the only person's opinion he really cared for was Griff's, and Griff was holding his hand, talking to him steadily in a quiet voice. Griff made him feel grounded in a good way, stable and loved. Griff paid attention to him, not because Blaze was bad or required monitoring, but because he wanted to *see* Blaze. It was an addicting thing to experience.

He and Griff led the way, using the suns for guides rather than the map. Blaze wasn't even sure if they were still looking for Griff's wings, or if they were now on a search for the truth about Ahndwa's claim— secretly, he thought Griff was the son of the goddess. Blaze could see the similarity in their features more and more, but he'd wait to discuss that with Griff when they wouldn't be overheard. It was clear by the way Griff had shut Jade's questions down earlier that Griff didn't want to discuss that matter with the others. Blaze was fairly certain Griff would want to talk to him about it.

But when they came to a rest for the night, when Griff led him away from the others, to a copse of trees bearing fragrant flowers and ripe, golden fruits, it wasn't conversation that Griff had in mind.

"Later," Griff said, his voice rough and low. "We can talk about it all later. For now, as funny as it may seem, I just want to forget about everything but you, and me, together here."

Griff cupped Blaze's cheek. "Nothing else matters right now, in this moment. It's just us, hidden from the outside world, with the moons and stars shining above."

He took Blaze's breath away. Never one to consider himself an intellectual, Blaze still got Griff's meaning. "Only us," he agreed before dipping his head just enough to show how much he wanted a kiss from his bonded.

In an instant, their clothes were gone, Griff having performed his magic without even needing the chant he'd used before. "Only us," Griff repeated, the words spoken against Blaze's lips before Griff sealed their mouths together.

Blaze dropped the pack he'd been holding and wrapped his arms around Griff. The warm, silky skin over finely sculpted muscles added more fuel to the fire of Blaze's arousal. His cock grew harder with every thrust of Griff's tongue, every nip of his teeth.

Blaze whimpered when Griff embraced him in return, holding Blaze by the nape and one shoulder.

Then Griff turned his head and trailed nipping kisses down to Blaze's neck before biting him just below the ear, the sting and ache making Blaze tremble.

"Gods," he rasped, running his hands down to Griff's ass. He cupped the firm mounds, kneading and warming up Griff's skin.

Now that he had his abilities back, Blaze's body temperature ran hotter. He thought Griff liked it, judging by the way the man was grinding on him and murmuring sweetly to him.

Blaze dared to dip his fingers into Griff's crease. He wasn't sure how far Griff would let him go there, but he wanted to touch his bonded so very badly.

Griff gasped and bit down harder on Blaze's shoulder. He curled his fingers against Blaze's skin, pricking it with blunt nails.

Blaze was going to shake so hard his bones popped right out of his body if Griff did that one-two combo again. "Griff, fuck me, please," he begged, forgetting about the barely realized desire to experiment with his bonded.

Griff, however, seemed to have other ideas. He scraped his teeth over Blaze's skin and arched his lower back, pushing his butt against Blaze's hands. "Not yet."

Blaze tingled from head to toe as his need ramped higher. "Can I...?" He trailed off as he dared to move his fingers down to the tight little hole nestled between Griff's cheeks.

Griff tugged on Blaze's neck. "Down. Lie down with me."

Blaze and Griff stretched out on the ground, made soft by the thick grass. He rolled to his back and pulled Griff on top of him. Their kisses grew fiercer as Blaze eased one of Griff's ass cheeks aside so he could finger his hole.

Griff wiggled and rocked on top of Blaze, grinding against Blaze's cock. Griff pressed a hand to Blaze's jaw suddenly and pushed his head up. The change in position exposed Blaze's neck to Griff.

Blaze nudged the tip of one finger against Griff's entrance. Without lube, he wouldn't use more than just the one, but Griff might not even want that.

Except Griff mewled and rocked back just before latching on to Blaze's neck. He sucked strongly and wiggled his butt again.

Blaze pressed into the snug heat, and his eyes rolled back as he imagined it gripping his cock. "Griff," he got out as Griff's ring tightened around his finger.

Griff scraped his nails over Blaze's shoulders while he sucked up a mark on his neck.

Blaze held still, wanting to do so many things at once, he couldn't do any of them. He had his finger in to the first knuckle, he wanted a kiss, wanted more biting, more sucking and fucking and touching—

When Griff sat up and forced Blaze's finger in deeper, Blaze remembered the pack. "The—" was as far as he got before Griff arched and began fucking himself on that finger.

"Fuck," Blaze whispered, stunned by the erotic picture Griff made. A moment later, Griff leaned forward and pinched both of Blaze's nipples. Blaze's shout scared the sleeping birds from the nearby trees.

Griff did it again as he moved his hips, pinching and twisting Blaze's nipples until they were throbbing, swollen, and he feared he'd come from the torment.

"Griff," he got out between panted breaths, "I'll come if you keep it up."

"It's that good?" Griff asked, stilling all movements.

"'S that good," Blaze answered. "And I want—I need you."

Griff clenched, and Blaze got the message, withdrawing his finger.

"You have me," Griff said. He stretched and reached for the bag.

When he had a palmful of lubricant, Blaze expected him to get up so he could lube Blaze's hole.

But Griff startled him to no end by rising up enough to slather the lubricant on Blaze's cock.

"Griff?" Blaze asked, his voice cracking. "Are you sure?"

Griff winked at him, then turned to straddle him backward, delighting and arousing Blaze even more, because he got to watch Griff push two slick fingers into his own hole.

Blaze's nipples flared with heat, and he had to get his hands on Griff's ass. He held Griff's cheeks apart as Griff worked his pucker, stretching it and getting it ready for Blaze.

Blaze let go of one cheek to palm Griff's heavy balls instead. He rolled them and pressed them up to Griff's body as Griff moaned.

"Help me," Griff said.

Blaze frowned. "How?"

Griff looked back at him. "Put a finger in with mine."

"Fuck yes!" Blaze felt like a virgin with his enthusiasm shining so bright, but everything he did with Griff was new because of the emotions and bond they shared. He wouldn't have dared to let anyone else see him so eager for anything.

Blaze ran his thumb through the slick fluid around Griff's hole. When Griff went to shove his own fingers in, Blaze pressed until his thumb joined them. It'd been tight before, but now it was even more so.

"Griff, if it's too much, tell me," he said, unwilling to risk hurting his bonded.

"More," Griff demanded. "Give it to me!"

Blaze pushed in deeper, watching the way Griff's ring stretched to accommodate their combined digits. He wished then he'd used a finger so he could have reached Griff's gland, but he hadn't.

Griff groaned and rocked back. "Out. Get it out. I want to ride your cock."

Blaze was careful. He was, but Griff yanked his fingers free as if something were chasing them. The idea made Blaze giggle, but only for a second, because then Griff was ordering him to hold his dick up.

Blaze held it at the base, and Griff lined up, his hole right against Blaze's tip. Blaze wished Griff would turn around. He wanted to stare into Griff's eyes.

But Griff was in control. He sat up and sank down on Blaze's cock with one slow, steady movement, taking Blaze in to the hilt.

Blaze tried to say something intelligent, like, "Gods, that feels *so* fucking amazing!" but it all came out as a garbled jumble of letters with no discernible connection.

He ran his hands up and down Griff's back and ass, then Griff rose up and clenched tight around Blaze's cockhead.

Blaze forgave himself for squeaking. He was close to losing his damned mind from the pleasure of being in Griff like he was.

Griff rocked back down, then set up a hard, fast pace, his balls slapping against Blaze's in a way that ramped up the need spiraling through Blaze.

Blaze planted his heels and thrust up, driving into the silky, tight heat of Griff's ass over and over. He keened when Griff scratched his thighs, the slight pain emphasizing the ecstasy he felt.

Blaze kept one hand on Griff, but brought the other to his own chest, where he worked at his nipples, sore as they were. He had so much feeling inside, so much rapture and bliss, that he had to bring the pain along with it. The two things seemed to feed off each other, and his body was a riot of stunning sensations he'd never imagined existed.

Then Griff pulled off, and before Blaze could process that, Griff was straddling him again, facing him, getting right back on Blaze's shaft.

Blaze shouted, his throat aching as Griff drove down on him. Griff slapped Blaze's hand from his breast and bent, raking the sore nub with his teeth. Blaze bucked and grabbed on to Griff's hips. He shoved up into Griff's hole a dozen times in quick order, his balls aching and tingling with the promise of release.

Griff moved unlike any sexual partner Blaze had ever had. His hips were in constant motion as he rode

Blaze's cock in a smooth, fast rhythm that never faltered.

Not until Blaze gripped Griff's hips and slammed him down, hard enough to bruise them both. Blaze jerked from head to toe as he shouted, spunk jetting from his cock. He had no more restraint. Griff had ridden it out of him.

Griff clenched, and his inner walls milked Blaze's dick until Blaze whimpered and went lax beneath Griff.

Then Griff let Blaze's cock slip free. Blaze blinked until he could see—once he realized opening his eyes would help, it went better—and he felt his dick twitch as Griff reached back at his own hole.

When Griff then used the mixture of lube and cum to jerk off with, Blaze thought he'd pass out from the fresh wave of lust that hit him. He wanted... everything.

"Wait," he ground out, wrapping his hand around Griff's wrist. "Fuck me now?"

Griff was very close, but he nodded once. "On your belly. Can you take me if I go slow? Just my cock?"

Blaze really needed to work on the whimpering thing. He wouldn't, though. He liked letting Griff know how badly he *wanted.*

No sooner was Blaze on his belly than Griff was pressing his fat cock to Blaze's hole. "Be still," Griff growled.

"M'kay." Blaze closed his eyes and bit his lip. It hurt at first, when Griff's tip penetrated him. Then Blaze moaned and tipped his butt up as that burn was chased with pleasure.

Griff never said a word. He was reduced to panting and grunting as he bottomed out.

Blaze wiggled enough to let him know it was good, very good, then Griff didn't hold back any longer. He drove his cock into Blaze's ass harder and harder, each thrust driving Blaze forward on the grass.

Blaze would have come up to his knees, but Griff shoved his hands under Blaze and grabbed his shoulders. He controlled Blaze's body, held it still for the taking and for the giving.

All Blaze could do was moan and feel. His dick was hard again, and with nothing more than the ground beneath him, he wouldn't be able to get off.

Or so he thought until Griff bit his nape. The climax blindsided Blaze. He might have screamed, might have been silent. He didn't know because his thoughts exploded into chaos as he came, enveloped in the intensity of his orgasm.

Griff slammed in once more, and Blaze felt every shot of Griff's cum splattering inside him, marking him.

Griff held still, then after a moment, he ground against Blaze's ass. He rose up, pressing his hands to Blaze's shoulders, pinning him down.

And Blaze felt it, the need still there between them.

Griff *needed* him, needed an escape from the fear and worry, to know he was loved and cherished, that Blaze would be there for him, always. That feeling was manifesting in a physical form, but that wasn't all there was to it. Their bond was strengthening, their love expanding.

Talking would wait.

Chapter Thirty-Four

"It's like the world keeps turning faster than we're walking, and it's sending us off on the wrong course with every step we take," Griff said, tired after a sleepless night and a hard day of traveling.

"Perhaps it would be wise to discuss who might have the power to fuck with you this way." Jade's voice was heavy with sarcasm. "You know, like I've suggested us doing this morning."

"Maybe if you weren't such an ass about it, we'd have done that," Blaze snapped. "Why is it royalty thinks it's fine to talk to regular people like they're shit?"

Jade sniffed. "Please. If Griff is the son of a goddess, he outranks me. Which doesn't mean he shouldn't have listened to me sooner."

Griff wanted to snarl and snap at Jade. The fact was, he knew Jade was right, but the Storm King annoyed him to no end with his haughty attitude.

And, admittedly, Griff was afraid of what answers they might come up with if they brainstormed on the situation.

He didn't want to believe that Gia and the rest of the fairies he'd known had all lied to him. His own parents—or not his own, if the deceit had been truly deep—had lied. That meant everything Griff had thought he knew was wrong. Considering his memory issues, that possibility terrified him.

But they were lost, because the suns *had* begun to move across the sky faster than they were supposed to be moving, and such an event could only be possible through a powerful illusion.

"This might not be about me," he felt compelled to point out, glaring at Jade. "You're the one on the run from the other evil elves."

"*Other* evil elves?" Jade crossed his arms over his narrow chest as his eyes gleamed with anger. "Are you saying that *I'm* evil?"

"Well, you did take years off Grlind's life," Blaze pointed out.

"Now wait just a minute," Grlind began, only to be cut off by Jade.

"I didn't take those from him! And if I had the power to give them back to him, I would," Jade said. "Every moment he gave me, I would return, but I can't." Jade turned to look directly at Grlind. "I owe you an unimaginable debt. I will find a way to repay it."

Grlind shook his head. "No. I won't accept."

Jade stomped over to the orc, shaking a finger at him. "You *will not* refuse a gift of payment from the Storm King!"

Blaze tugged on Griff's wrist. Heat flared between them as Griff looked into Blaze's eyes. Images from their lovemaking the night before flitted through Griff's mind. That part of the sleepless night had been amazing. He didn't regret anything about it, and in fact, felt the warmth of arousal beginning in his groin.

"We don't have to talk with them if you aren't ready," Blaze said, pulling Griff closer.

Griff shook his head. "No. As much as I hate to admit it, Jade's right, and this...this situation is growing direr." He ran a hand through his hair. "That's not the word I want. I can't think of it. But it's — Oh! It's escalating! It must take a great deal of power to commit such a hallucination. This can't be happening to everyone in our world, so it must not be real."

"Oh, are we discussing this now?"

Griff gritted his teeth, biting back a growl. He didn't know why Jade was bugging him so much more today than before.

Then again—Griff glanced at Grlind, who was obviously angry, his green skin a mottled, ugly gray on his cheeks and neck. He was scowling hard enough to turn Medusa into stone. Jade was still irritated as well, and Griff wasn't himself—

He turned back to Blaze. "Do you feel angry? Grouchy? Not exactly yourself?"

Blaze frowned. "Jade bugs me as much as he always has." He shrugged.

"What are you thinking?" Jade asked.

"That it's odd how angry three of us are," Griff answered. "If Blaze was feeling it, too, I'd think we were bespelled."

Jade cocked his head, narrowing his eyes as he considered what Griff had said. After a moment, he said, "Not all spells work on all species."

Griff darted a glance up at the sky. "Surely a deity would know that, though," he whispered, as if that would keep the gods from hearing him. "If it were a deity casting the spell?"

Jade snorted, and while he didn't answer, his expression made it clear that he didn't think the gods were all that bright. Not every one of them, at least.

"We could just be tired and stressed. As to spells...there are others besides gods with great powers," Grlind contributed. "Wizards, warlocks, witches—and why do they all start with a w, do you think?"

Jade rolled his eyes. "That hardly matters. What's important is that Griff is the son of a favored goddess, and his entire frolic has to know he isn't one of them. At least his king and family must know."

"I might not be the son of Ahndwa," Griff protested. "I don't feel like a demigod. Or a full-blooded god. I don't feel like anything other than a very confused fairy!" And he was so tired of it. "Surely if I carried the blood of Ahndwa in my veins, I would know it."

Wouldn't I?

Chapter Thirty-Five

"Maybe, if we all pool our powers, we can do...something," Griff finished, flailing his arms as if to chase off the uncertainty in his voice.

"What powers?" Grlind asked. "I'm just an orc. I can't breathe fire or control the weather or chant and bring magic out of my body."

Griff sent him a sweet little smile that warmed Blaze just to see it.

"Magic out of my body?" Griff asked of Grlind.

Blaze happened to know for a fact that Griff's body was overflowing with magic, albeit probably not the kind the other two men were talking about. But Blaze believed there was something to sex magic, and Griff had it. He could enslave Blaze easily with his loving, though Griff would never do such a thing.

Of course, Blaze had willingly given Griff his heart, but Griff had his in return.

"Pay attention, Smoky," Jade grumbled.

Blaze turned his head enough to glower at the Storm King. "Shut up, Flash."

"Flash?" Jade blinked. "Oh. You mean like lightning."

Blaze could have been mean and said no, like gone in a flash, as in toppled in a coup, but even he wasn't that snarky. "Yeah. Or I could just call you Hail. Or Puddle. Oh, Puddle would work."

"I can have a lightning bolt hit you in the ass," Jade threatened, sparks dancing over his fingertips.

"Are you two done sniping?" Grlind asked. "Ready to listen to Griff's plan?"

"How did — ?" Blaze shook his head. "How did we miss a whole plan that quick?"

"As much as I'd like to tell you that yes, you were too busy bickering to hear what I was saying, it wouldn't be the truth, but I *did* mention the plan before that — us pooling our powers," Griff said. "And despite what anyone else might think, every creature living in our world has magical powers. We *are* magical beings. It flows through us and creates us, sustains us. None of us are without it."

Grlind's eyebrows were nestled together as he frowned, but Blaze thought Griff was right.

"You are a treasure," Jade told Griff.

And apparently, the Storm King knew it, too.

Jade patted Griff's back. "I have always had a thing for intellectuals. Too bad you're taken."

Blaze growled, but Jade flicked his fingers at him. "Please. I'm not interested in taking your man. I was only praising him for being useful. Isn't that what a good king or queen would do? I know you don't think much of royalty, Blaze, but really, I try to do better, and you look like you want to singe me."

"Doing better and handing out praise doesn't mean flirting," Grlind explained while Blaze still struggled with getting a word out past the rage knotting his throat. "Jade, stop being a prick. If you're into intellectuals, try to act intelligently yourself."

"Why—" Jade flushed dark, anger rolling over him like the clouds rolled up in the sky. "You big ignorant oaf! You can't speak to me like that!"

Grlind scowled. "I just did, and now you're going to have a temper tantrum like a babe who didn't get his way. Very kingly."

"It actually is," Blaze muttered as thunder clapped loud enough to make his ears ring.

"Stop it!" Griff shouted. "Stop arguing! We're being manipulated and fighting will be playing into the hands of whoever's trying to pull our strings."

"And who might that be?" Jade asked after taking a deep breath.

Griff bit his bottom lip until Blaze saw a speck of blood well up, the dark red contrasting vibrantly against the white of Griff's teeth.

"Don't." Blaze thumbed Griff's lip. "You're hurting yourself." He swiped at the small hurt.

Griff shivered, his eyes huge as he looked at Blaze. "My king has to be involved," Griff whispered. "He can't be ignorant of what we're doing now. He's had to have found out we left to find my wings, and that you're my bonded."

"Why should he care?" Blaze asked. "He wanted you in his harem, but he has more people in it than he has time for fucking. Sorry," he tacked on quickly. "No offense to your sister."

"No, I know you didn't mean anything bad toward her." Griff brushed a few strands of hair off his cheek. "I still don't think Gia is involved. She helped us, and

Artaxis... He might have wanted me in his harem for reasons other than because he found me desirable."

"Like that you're the son of a goddess?" Jade asked.

Griff shook his head. "I don't know if I am, and that's the most I can admit to right now. I don't *feel* like I am. I'm still just...just me. That doesn't mean I'm not—her son, I mean. I just don't know."

At least Griff was keeping an open mind about it.

Jade nodded curtly. "All right then. So you believe your king is involved. Is he powerful enough to do this?" He gestured to their surroundings. "Create an illusion so great we can't tell it's an illusion?"

"I thought he was just a fairy king," Griff said. "What do I truly know of his powers? Nothing. He could also be working with other, more powerful people. But to what end?"

"It's always something stupid like wanting to take over the world because they got their feelings hurt when they were rebuffed by a crush," Blaze pointed out, not really joking. "Something little that makes someone crack, and they crave power." *Like Bonny. Oh shit! Like Bonny!* He turned to Griff. "Bonny. She is powerful. I don't know how much, how strong, but she's definitely powerful, and she'd be pissed that I got to have you, that I have a bonded. She wouldn't like it that I'm happy, I don't think. Or she'd at least be jealous."

"And maybe scared that Fyre might find a bond mate of his own, and leave her," Griff mused. "Still, what would any of that have to do with me being Ahndwa's son, if I am?"

"She could be a seer," Jade offered. "One who can detect power and magic."

"Such people exist?" Griff only grunted when Jade assured him they did.

"There's no telling why anyone is after us. We'll only get answers if we find the people or person responsible," Grlind added. "So perhaps we should do that. Griff said combine our magic." He looked up at the sky. "When the moons are centered, that would be when we are strongest, correct?"

"The magic time, yes." Jade sighed. "What do we do? Join hands and dance around naked?"

"Not a bad idea, but no," Griff told him. "Although, there is powerful magic in sex. But no. No orgy will take place tonight. But we will do what we must. Sex, blood, sacrifice — those all strengthen magic. Blaze and I can take care of the first and —"

"And no," Jade cut in. "I mean, yes to that part, but Grlind has already sacrificed, more than anyone should have ever done, or would have ever done, for me. So that leaves only me to contribute, and we need blood. The blood of the Storm King should be quite a gift to give. Gods know there's plenty of people who'd love to see it spilled."

Chapter Thirty-Six

"This is a little, er, different." Blaze just *knew* he was blushing all over with embarrassment.

Or arousal. He didn't want to examine the cause too closely.

Griff caressed his cheek. "Are you sure you want to do this?" he asked in a low voice meant only for Blaze to hear.

Blaze cast a quick look at Grlind and Jade, who were having their own two-person conference several feet away. Neither of them appeared to be happy, and he thought they were bickering. Jade was gesturing animatedly with his hands while Grlind's expression grew dourer by the second.

"We can come up with another way," Griff continued, now framing Blaze's face in his hands. "We don't have to do this. Sex magic is something Love fairies are good at, yes, but if I'm not a Love fairy, this might all be for naught."

"Sex magic isn't just a Love fairy thing," Blaze pointed out. "It's the intent that counts, too, not just the bloodlines." He leaned in and took a quick kiss. "I'm fine. I'm actually—" Blaze had to clear his throat to get the admission out. "Kind of turned on. From knowing. You know. That they'll be watching us."

Griff's eyebrows shot up his forehead, and his eyes rounded. "Really?" He ran his hands down Blaze's chest, beyond his belly, farther south until he was fondling Blaze's cock. "Hm. Not hard."

"Yet," Blaze grumped out. "Not hard *yet*." But even in that short period of time, his shaft had begun to firm up. "Anything you want to do, anything, I'm all for." He meant it. Griff could fuck him, suck him, jack him, all three, other things, any combo— "Anything. I'm yours. I'm ready."

Griff's delight showed in the smile he gave Blaze. "Let's see what we feel like doing once we begin."

"Which will be…" Blaze glanced up at the sky. The moons were still off to the east. "Ugh. Too long."

Griff chuckled and moved one hand down to palm Blaze's balls. "A couple of hours, yes. I wonder if I can keep you hard that long?"

Blaze groaned. Griff probably could—and would—do just that.

As much as Griff had wanted to keep Blaze hard until it was time for their magic, he had to intervene on the fighting that broke out between Jade and Grlind. Once he got them calmed down, he checked the moons' positions.

Part of sex magic was in the fluidity and connection made between those involved in the act. Orgies were strong conductors of magic, when the group could focus on the power they brought out.

He wasn't willing to go that far, not if it meant sharing his bonded.

If Grlind and Jade decided to make an...additional...contribution to the magic, then so be it. Griff couldn't imagine them doing anything with one another, but masturbating wasn't out of the question.

He'd be too busy with Blaze to pay any attention anyway.

The air carried with it a definite hint of foreboding. Griff felt it blow in, a supernaturally chilly sensation that had him glancing at Jade with an unspoken question.

Jade shook his head. "That's not me. That's...that's evil."

"Even I can feel it," Grlind said, rubbing his arms. "Someone isn't willing to wait for us to begin."

"No, they aren't," Griff whispered, noticing dark shapes rippling through the trees, coming their way. "Look!"

"They hope to stall us so we must wait another night?" Jade muttered. "I don't think so!" He raised his arms, and his eyes rolled back until only the whites showed. Lightning swirled in the sky a moment later, a tornadic show of the Storm King's power.

Except it wasn't just for show. Jade's lips moved, the sound that left them that of s gusting through anything that stood in their way. He had said that Grlind had given him too much, and Griff wondered if this was a result of that.

The power Jade was giving off was incredible, and it wasn't until Grlind shouted that Griff saw it — blood running down Jade's arms from his wrists. Only the fact that the blood wasn't flowing thick or gushing reassured Griff that Jade hadn't gone too far with his sacrifice.

And if Jade was starting the magic early, so would they. While having the moons overhead just so was the ideal, it wasn't absolutely necessary.

"Watch over Jade," Griff shouted to Grlind as the noise increased. The pressure in the air made Griff's ears ache, and he had to grit his teeth to counter it.

Whatever was coming for them was about to get blasted. Every hair on Griff's body stood up as Jade's voice grew as loud as a thousand storms.

Griff grabbed Blaze and wrapped his arms around him. "Now!" He gripped Blaze's nape and used the hold to bring Blaze's head closer.

"But—" Blaze began, trying to turn around.

"No! We can't let them win!" He wasn't sure who or what he was talking about, only that the words wouldn't be held back. Griff growled as he tussled with Blaze in an erotic shuffle, the pursuit of pleasure a goal not secondary to the magic it would inspire.

He wanted Blaze, with every particle of his being. More than he'd ever wanted him.

And Blaze wasn't fighting to get away. He was struggling to get closer, to get more of Griff.

Griff clipped Blaze's left heel, catching it with his own foot and tumbling Blaze to the ground. He was on Blaze in less than a heartbeat, crushing their mouths together as thunder shook the ground. Great flashes of lightning were followed by otherworldly shrieks. Whatever was out there in the trees had met the first blows of Jade's powers.

Blaze panted and arched under him, bucking, feeding their mutual desire with rough hands and rougher thrusts.

Griff bit him, leaving a line of red marks from Blaze's jaw to his clavicle. Magic thrummed through Griff, through Blaze. Despite the turmoil around them, Griff's focus narrowed down to Blaze and the need they shared.

Chapter Thirty-Seven

Blaze felt the magic swelling in him, pulsing between him and Griff and filling the air around them. The tingling heat that spiraled through his body when Griff thrust into him was unlike anything he'd ever known before. Blaze could only assume that same magic made it possible for Griff to push into him so easily, without hurting Blaze at all.

It was almost too intense, the power too great, the intimacy a deeper level even as he felt exposed to the world.

Blaze locked gazes with Griff. In his eyes, he saw a myriad of colors, images so fleeting Blaze couldn't make them out. They moved like clouds in the depths of Griff's eyes, and Blaze shivered with the surety that there was much more to Griff than any of them knew.

Then Griff kissed him, and at the same time, thrust his cock in the last few inches. Blaze's lips parted on a gasp and a moan. His pleasure centers went haywire as Griff drove his thick shaft into Blaze's ass again and again.

Blaze could do nothing but feel. He tried to get his hands and legs to move, and maybe they did. Maybe he was able to wrap them around Griff and hold on to him like he wanted to.

Every thrust, every grunt and slap of flesh on flesh, incited more rough need in Blaze. He wanted every bite and nip, every hard grasp and deep penetration.

Griff raised his head, ending the kiss, and still, Blaze couldn't close his eyes. Griff's gaze held him entranced as the electric charge of their mating sizzled between them.

There were no screams, no storm, only muted sounds as Blaze's focus was on his bonded and himself. He heard their breaths, their moans, their curses and vows, words he knew and ones he didn't spilling from his lips as fast as they appeared in his mind.

A great light surrounded him and Griff, then Blaze's vision dimmed under a mighty wave of rapturous pleasure. He arched and keened as he came, Griff's hand suddenly on his cock, working it with harsh strokes.

Barely a moment later, Griff's broken breath had Blaze's focus centering on him. Griff's skin seemed to glow, tiny beads of sweat glistening on his brow as he drove in harder and harder. His full lips thinned, and the cords in his neck stood out. His hair swirled around them, caught by the wind or something magical.

Griff's eyes still held those secrets, those fleeting images, until the moment his climax tore through him. His pupils expanded and chased out everything else, every hint of any other color. Griff bared his teeth and strained against Blaze, as if trying to get closer, deeper, and Blaze whimpered when he felt the hot jets of Griff's cum inside him.

The howling that followed was otherworldly, and it came from neither Griff nor Blaze. It tore away their solitude, and Blaze found himself holding on to Griff tightly while Griff's body was jerked back by invisible forces.

The separation of their bodies was uncomfortable, but Blaze ignored the pain as he pulled against whatever force was trying to lift Griff away. "You can't have him! You *can't*!" He used his whole body to keep a hold on Griff as Griff's feet left the ground.

Blaze ignored the pummeling against his back as he was jerked to his feet. He dug his heels into the ground and curled around Griff, letting his shift come swiftly. As a dragon, he weighed so much more and perhaps stood a better chance of protecting Griff.

Blaze roared and looked for a target for his anger, but there was nothing tangible for him to blast with fire. Jade was battling some sort of dark force, and Grlind had his hands full with daemons—and those, Blaze could do something about.

He let loose a stream of fire even while burrowing his claws into the ground. Blaze said a prayer to the earth, asking for help and protection. Whatever was trying to pull Griff away was powerful, more so than a fairy king or a cranky dragon queen. Even combined, Blaze didn't think they could do what was being done.

Not when Jade was so strong, and he was struggling. Not when the world had been altered either truly or magically. Not when a goddess appeared and handed him a sword and called Griff *son*.

Blaze toasted the daemons and hoped that would allow Grlind to help Jade, because he had to concentrate on Griff.

And Griff needed to free his mind of the constraints on it and remember who he truly was.

Blaze turned his head and stared at Griff with one eye, willing him to reach into the depths of his mind for the truth. Whether he'd ever known it or not, it was there. Griff was extraordinary, and it was time for him to realize it. The how, the why, the what, exactly, were things Blaze couldn't accurately guess at, but he didn't need to.

He just needed his bonded to break the walls someone had built inside him. Blaze's paws left the ground as the force tugging at Griff grew stronger.

Please, Griff. Please. Blaze hoped his bonded understood the low rumble. He hoped Griff heard it. The pummeling along Blaze's back had become harsher, painful, as he'd shifted forms.

Find yourself. Find yourself, my bonded. If I could do it for you, I would.

Griff stared back at him, eyes black, mouth open, face so pale Blaze could see the fine blue veins under the skin.

A hard yank sent him and Griff to the ground again, but Blaze never lost his hold, never unfurled from around Griff.

Not even when the pummeling turned to something sharper, something agonizing. Blaze tried to ignore it, merely grunted and jerked a little, but the pain increased and spread from his spine to his sides, up his neck and down his tail. He was burning inside in a way that wasn't natural, that had nothing to do with his fire and his powers.

Try as he might, Blaze couldn't keep back the shriek that had built up in him. He feared he was dying, feared he'd let Griff down, had killed them both by being too weak—whatever was happening to him, he couldn't fight it off, not while he was keeping Griff from being taken away.

The buzzing in Blaze's ears had to be a sign of his impending death, the reaper coming for him. Blaze tried to swing his head around and see what was on him. He found himself staring at hundreds of tiny eyes and sparkling wings.

Dragonflies! Shadnay had returned with what looked to be the entire species of dragonflies, and as one, they swooped behind Blaze.

The pain didn't completely go away, but it decreased significantly as something screeched. Griff was shouting, his words foreign to Blaze, but the intent clear enough. He was inside himself, Blaze suspected, as another strong pull sent them in the direction he didn't want to go.

The tugging changed suddenly, with Blaze's arms being jerked sharply while his tail and back legs were pulled in the opposite direction. Whoever was doing it was trying to pull him apart, or enough so that he'd let go of Griff.

Blaze threw his head back and burned everything he could reach. He knew Jade and Grlind were out of range, and the dragonflies were behind him. Griff was still in his clutches, and Blaze's fire might have done no good at all, but it helped him in some way he couldn't name. Blaze drew strength from the fire, from his anger and pain and fear. He curled into a tighter ball around Griff and rolled with him, protecting his bonded from his own weight.

It hurt terribly. Whatever had been done to his back was a physical wound, not a psychic one. Blaze knew that much. The dragonflies swarmed over him and

Griff, a cloud of darkness and glittery wings trying to keep them safe.

Griff was still speaking, words that sounded ancient and unlike anything Blaze had ever heard. He was dimly aware of shouts and thunder, of Grlind's deep voice, of the answering yell from Jade and the *buzz-buzz-buzz* of the dragonflies.

That outside force pulling at him started up again, curling over his forearms and tail with icy talons that sank into his flesh. It was worse than before, the cold sucking away his internal fire in steady increments.

Griff vibrated in his arms, like a mighty bell rung, a sound leaving him that was both musical and eerie.

Days, weeks, years, centuries and more flashed through Blaze's mind. Something was changing, a new power swelling, emerging in the battle. He tried to cover Griff's head better, but Griff shook harder, and heat poured off him into Blaze.

It took a moment for Blaze to realize the new heat chased away the icy cold that had been filling him. It chased it away and restoked his own fire. The pain along Blaze's back ebbed to nothing more than a faint ache, and he felt stronger than he could ever remember being.

And Griff looked at him, then smiled and stroked Blaze's muzzle and spoke in that unknown tongue.

Blaze didn't let go of him, but Griff was free, standing in front of him and turning away from Blaze.

Blaze bellowed and tried to snatch him up again but failed when Griff spun aside. Griff glanced at him and shook his head. *Trust me.*

Blaze heard it as clear as could be in his head. He wavered, but when it came down to it, he *did* trust Griff and he trusted the bond between them.

And everything around them was chaos and bizarre and scary as all Hades. Griff was love and safety and home.

Blaze bobbed his head and moved to stand at Griff's side—which was where he should be, not covering Griff as if Griff were weak. Blaze got that now, and Griff seemed to have found some missing part of himself.

As soon as Blaze thought it, Griff flung his arms up and out. Flames and ice came at them, but between Blaze's own fire and Griff doing something magical that deflected several of the would-be weapons, he and Griff averted the attack.

Blaze recognized the fire of his kind. While he couldn't see the dragon firing at them, he knew it definitely *was* a dragon. Someone had used a powerful cloaking spell to hide behind, and he had a feeling he knew which dragon was trying to fry him and Griff. The ice, he had no clue as to who could manipulate such a thing. He didn't have time to dwell on it, either.

Griff pulled down his hands and in them were thin, beautiful pieces of material. They shimmered with pastels and silver threads, and mesmerized Blaze for a few seconds, which almost resulted in him getting a nasty ice ball to the head.

He ducked and blew flames out to protect himself and Griff.

Griff shook the material out, then wrapped it around his shoulders.

It was then that Blaze understood what he was seeing. *Wings.* Griff had his wings.

Chapter Thirty-Eight

Magic pulsed through Griff as if he were merely a vessel or conduit. Griff had felt it beginning when he was making love to Blaze. It had filled him to capacity and forced him to open his mind to it or be obliterated by the force of it.

Griff had given over after an internal struggle that had terrified him almost as much as the external struggle around them.

Then it had come — the knowledge of who he was — son of Ahndwa and the former Love fairy king, Xelscior, who had vanished long ago.

And who hadn't only been a fairy himself. Dark magic ran through Griff's veins, along with the power of a goddess. Xelscior's contribution to Griff's existence wasn't pure.

Even a goddess can fall for a bad boy. Griff would have been amused had he not been on the verge of losing his sanity. Too many things were happening in his mind. Visions, memories — his own, from this life and ones before, some he didn't believe were his at any point —

mysterious words and images worked through him. Griff stopped fighting and let the magic take over.

It illuminated every part of him. Griff felt like he could conquer anyone and anything that got in his way, though he knew that wasn't so. It was the discovery of a new strength, a secret embedded in his soul and bound by magic and a curse and fear itself.

Griff had to envision himself prying layer after layer of deceit away until he reached the epitome of who and what he was.

Son of a goddess, son of a dark fairy.

A combination that would ensure he'd be feared and perhaps even hunted.

And someone had likely done both.

It'd been a mighty hand that had swatted him down. Mightier than a dragon or normal magical being.

There was an oddly familiar tinge to the icy cold tendrils of magic in the air. The fire was from a dragon—and one he'd bet he knew. The cold…that was from someone else.

Someone stronger.

Someone he should recognize.

Griff would bet whoever was lobbing the deadly balls of ice at him and Blaze was the same person who had snatched his wings.

And that would take power. "Dark power," he murmured as he deflected another round of fire and ice.

Beside him, Blaze roared, and shadow figures shrieked before dissipating into gray wisps of steam.

Griff raised his hands up and called to the magic in him. He called to Ahndwa. As he did, his past replayed—he'd been bespelled and bound by a curse for so long, and when he'd begun to free himself of it, when he'd realized that he didn't fit in with his frolic and never would, he'd sought to leave. By finding a mate in another frolic, he'd have been out of the control of Artaxis —

Griff shuddered. Artaxis, his half-brother, his king and his would-be lover. Griff had never understood exactly why he had been so reluctant to give himself to Artaxis, but now he did. To some fairies, blood ties didn't preclude one from becoming a sexual partner, although it did for Griff. But did Artaxis know of their relation?

Griff had no answer for that. He saw himself leaving the frolic, felt his intent to be free because he didn't belong with them — and he saw it then, a tear in the fabric separating the worlds, the magical from the plain, a violent rend that shouldn't have existed.

From it came a blurred shape, and it seemed to stop as if surprised. Griff supposed that he wasn't expected, or at least not at that moment. He had left his frolic earlier than he'd told Artaxis he would, mainly because he'd been so eager to get away. So either he'd been about to be ambushed, or he'd come along when he shouldn't have. Either way, the end result had been the same.

That blurred form coalesced more clearly into a deep red shape, then again into the frame of a tall, thickly muscled man. He was beautiful, with very refined features and uptilted eyes. Griff barely got to see him before the man struck him with a wave of magic that had almost killed Griff. He heard cackling, laughter and a joyful promise to rip away his wings.

The agony had been so sharp that Griff had screamed and screamed and passed out, and he still didn't know who the man was who'd hurt him.

But he shivered as he realized the same man was there now. Someone strong enough to pass between the worlds, someone cruel enough to rip away his wings.

And twisted enough to hand them back to Griff now.

Griff had snatched them from the ether and nearly wept with the mixture of joy and fear — fear the wings would be snatched away from him before he could do more than touch their silky warmth.

Before the fear could paralyze him, the wings pulsed and a voice whispered to him, *It is I who have given your wings back to you, not he who took them.* Ahndwa's voice, telling him she'd taken what had been stolen from him, and she who returned them to him.

Griff lifted the wings and barely had to maneuver them at all before they were where they belonged. Pleasure, bright and beautiful, sang through his veins as his wings found their home again.

Beside him, Blaze bellowed, but it sounded more like a song than a raging protest.

Griff caressed Blaze with one wing and one hand. Sparkling currents of affection passed between him and his bonded even as another round of assaults began.

"We will not lose," Griff vowed.

"Gods, your wings are gorgeous," Jade rasped from behind Griff.

Griff swirled his hands, sending back the projectiles coming toward them. He spared a glance for Jade. "They are." He was maybe a little vain about his wings. They were like no other fairy's, and now he knew why.

Because he was the son of Ahndwa and blessed by the goddess. But even a demigod needed help, and friends.

Griff shouted for Grlind, and he held out a hand to Jade. "Form a circle. Blaze, shift. You can still use your fire, right?"

Jade threw a mighty gust of wind and hail toward their invisible attackers at the same time Blaze shifted.

Griff didn't have to give orders. As one, the four of them joined hands and formed their circle. "We have given, and taken, honored and worshipped. We have served and will serve. We have joined together now as one."

The rest of the words were of an old tongue, one carried through lifetimes. Griff heard his bonded and their friends repeating the words, then saying them along with Griff.

Their souls had met before, had fought beside one another, had laughed and cried with each other before. The pieces of their pasts bound them together for eternity, and Griff knew they'd fought noble causes every time they'd lived. Some they had won, some they had lost.

This time, they would prevail. "Name them," Griff demanded, his heart racing. "Name them, and they will show themselves."

"Bonny," Blaze growled. "Come forth!"

Griff saw it as if from an aerial view. His eyes saw something else, the world in shades of magic, in life and death. His thoughts were combined with Blaze's, Jade's and Grlind's. For now, they were as one. Their mind's eye saw the dragon queen ripped from the veil separating the worlds—something that shouldn't be possible.

Yet it was.

It would take a great power to move back and forth between the worlds.

A dark power to assault the son of a goddess.

A bitter soul to harm an innocent. Griff wasn't even sure who's thoughts they were, he only knew he heard them clearly.

But he knew without a doubt who it was when Ahndwa spoke to them. *One cast aside for trying to murder his own child. I hid you in plain sight, and even Artaxis did not know of your nature. Had Artaxis not appealed to the goddess Hetrexa to save you, you would have died when your wings were taken. Artaxis remembers none of that. Hetrexa saved you, and in doing so, had to alter his memories to save him as well. He would not have hesitated to go after the one who hurt you.*

Griff was relieved to learn that Artaxis was innocent, and puzzled by Artaxis's protectiveness, but then again, Artaxis was his king. He was strangely unhurt learning who had tried to destroy him.

Griff didn't hesitate at all to call out his father's name. "Xelscior!"

Bonny screamed and shifted, turning into a magnificent dragon. She came at them in full fury, her roar shaking the ground and her fire exploding all around them as Jade called forth the wind to fan the flames away.

"Xelscior! Stop hiding like a coward!" Griff pulled at the magic he and his circle wielded, drawing from it, pushing, tugging, trying to force the dark fairy to appear. For one moment, he considered whether he was wrong, but Ahndwa whispered in his ear and Griff knew he was right. Xelscior was very powerful, however, and he resisted being brought forth.

"Ahndwa, help us," Griff cried out, his entire body aching from the strain of trying to pull Xelscior to them.

I cannot. I am bound by a promise and must do no more to help you. Xelscior was once bound by his word, but he has given up his soul for power – and that is why he seeks your *soul, Griff. You are the one true son. Artaxis may be Xelscior's son, but it is only in name. Do not give up.* Ahndwa sounded sincere and regretful, which was great but didn't help at all.

"We will not lose," Blaze murmured, then repeated loudly. He squeezed Griff's hand. "Xelscior, come forth!"

Bonny screeched, coming off more like a giant rat than a dragon, but her furious display was eclipsed by the shout from Griff, Blaze, Grlind and Jade, calling out Xelscior. Their voices combined into a great, otherworldly sound that carried with it voices from lifetimes past.

Xelscior came through the fabric, shouting and leading a band of daemons and dragons.

The battle had truly begun.

Chapter Thirty-Nine

Xelscior's skin was a mottled red and gray, unlike any fairy Blaze had ever seen before. That Griff resembled the man was indisputable, but whereas Griff's features carried a lightness to them, Xelscior's were somehow tinged with evil. Of course, that could have just been Blaze's imagination. He didn't really have time to study the man, what with all the damned creatures coming at him and his friends—and Griff, who was glowing like a star in their midst.

In fact, Griff was sparkling, and it was as eerie as it was breathtakingly beautiful.

Griff's wings extended out to close to a dozen feet on either side of him. His hands held white-silver flames encapsulated in orange and blue fire. He was a mix of magics and strengths.

Blaze wanted to focus on him instead of the fact that Bonny was there, ordering daemons to come after him, lobbing her own fire and poisonous hatred at him.

She'd helped raise him, for gods' sakes. It hurt him to the core to have her turn on him in such a way.

And it would destroy Fyre.

Blaze had started to shift when something stopped him—a sizzle-pop of power shooting through him. Not a deadly one, nor an attack, but a familiar and welcomed one. In an instant, he held the Sword of Synchrony in his hands, and it sang to his blood as if it were a part of him. There was nothing awkward or wrong about how the sword fit in his grip now.

The sword deflected Bonny's fire and the current of electricity she sent at him. He swatted aside ice and daemons, sliced through them and filled the air with a fetid stench that overpowered the sulfur-fumes of dragon fire.

Griff was battling through the daemons and dragons that Xelscior kept sending his way. Jade shrieked as he sliced off a dragon's snout.

Blaze didn't know where Jade had gotten the sword he wielded nor did it matter. Jade was a deadly foe and Grlind was as well. Grlind threw back his head and roared, and the sound of it sent the closest daemons reeling back.

Blaze locked gazes with Bonny, still in her dragon form. She was beautiful, strikingly so, and he dreaded their confrontation, because only one of them would survive it.

And he would not be leaving Griff here to live out the rest of his days alone.

Blaze had always been afraid of Bonny. He'd mouthed off, certainly, but he'd been afraid of her. She'd known it, too. Maybe she hadn't always hated him, or maybe she had. Blaze wanted to think she'd been good once, and something had warped her over the past few years. He could remember a time when she laughed more than she scowled, when she'd reached for Fyre with tenderness instead of snapping at him with anger.

When she hadn't taken pleasure in hurting a young, orphaned dragon who couldn't control his fire or his shift. Somewhere between then and now, she'd changed, and he didn't know why.

He suspected the why of it was important.

If he had time to question her, that would have been great, but he didn't and doubted he would get any answers from her anyway.

He deflected a steady stream of flames from her, angling the sword so the fire shot off it and annihilated a half-dozen daemons and scorched a dragon that had been darting past to attack Jade.

Someone cackled gleefully, and he wasn't sure it wasn't one of the people on his side. There was a glory in a righteous war for some people. Blaze felt only utter sadness and firm determination. He locked up the pain of such a deep betrayal and focused on what he had to do.

Blaze only glanced away from Bonny to check on Griff as he cut through body after body. Gore splattered on him, and he ignored it, swiping off only what he had to to see and breathe clearly.

Then Griff was at Blaze's side and a little in front of him. Blaze could see Griff in his peripheral vision, but couldn't see Jade or Grlind. He heard them, though, both shouting with every victory as they battled.

Blaze felt stronger with each life he took, not something he was reveling in, but a side effect, he suspected, of the sword. It hadn't been like that when he'd killed the fiends, but fiends were odd creatures, and he'd already killed more daemons and dragons in the current battle than he had fiends. Perhaps the sword grew stronger with more blood spilled, or certain types of it. Blaze didn't know and couldn't dwell on it.

He hated taking a life, especially that of another dragon, and yet he did so without hesitation. It could mean the life of his bonded and their friends if he faltered.

At least none of the dragons but Bonny were known to him.

Bonny bellowed at him, her golden eyes narrowing as she backed up with his approach. If she took to the air, he'd have to shift, and the sword would be of no use then.

Griff was almost to Xelscior, who seemed unwilling to flee. The evil fairy was pulling up large, jagged clouds of something malevolent. Just seeing them made Blaze's skin crawl.

Bonny clawed at the ground and arched her neck, tossing her head as she sent more daemons his way. The dragons were either defecting from her command or going after reinforcements, Blaze wasn't sure which. He saw four of them shooting up into the sky and veering off to the north.

Whatever they were up to, he had to concentrate on Bonny. Blaze held the sword up and took out the daemons with it and an incredible flame he exhaled at them. Never had he been so skilled at warfare, nor in so much control of his abilities.

"What have you done?" he asked of Bonny as the ashes of her army fell to his feet. "What have you done!" he shouted, furious on Fyre's behalf. "You have betrayed him!" Which was worse than her betraying *him*, much worse.

Bonny didn't answer with anything other than a rough, cruel laugh. Coming from her as a dragon, the sound was otherworldly and sent a shiver down Blaze's spine.

He took a step toward her, every hair on his nape quivering with unease as he tried to guess her next move.

She leapt at him, her movement so sudden and without the warning of tensed muscles and flicked tail. Blaze sucked in a sharp breath and started to raise his sword.

Bonny shot up out of reach—all except for her deadly tail. Had he been a fraction of a second slower, he'd have been headless instead of shouting as he ducked and stumbled aside. The flat edge of her tail caught him on the head, stunning him for a moment, but not disabling him.

"Blaze!" Griff shouted.

Blaze's vision swam, but he shook his head and stood up, holding his weapon, ready to strike. He saw Bonny twenty feet past him.

"Blaze!" Griff shouted again, alarm making his voice strident.

Blaze jerked his attention from Bonny to Griff just as a dark, sharp object came at him. He swung the sword and hissed when Xelscior's magic, whatever it was, divided into numerous smaller projectiles. "Shit shit shit!" Blaze flamed and managed to get most of them, but a couple hit his chest and scored marks on his flesh.

The burning was not debilitating, the wounds not deep, but Griff's furious shout promised retribution for Blaze's pain.

Blaze plucked out the first of the odd spiked objects and tossed it aside. He had to leave the second one in as Bonny turned and dove right at him. Her flames were hotter and heavier than before and buried in them was a magic not her own. Blaze could sense it, and he knew she was being aided, most likely by Xelscior in some way.

She has always been his tool. She is not what she has presented herself to be. Bonny is not a true dragon – she is the concubine to Xelscior. The bitterness in Ahndwa's voice said there was more to the story than that, but now wasn't the time for it.

Blaze didn't question hearing her voice in his head – she'd chosen him to use the sword, after all, at least temporarily.

Even knowing Bonny wasn't what he'd thought her to be didn't lessen his anxiety at knowing he had to kill her. Blaze's heart pounded as he planted his heels in preparation of her attack.

The sword held back her fire and magic, but it couldn't do everything. She was soon close enough that her wings and tail were going to be able to harm him.

Blaze moved the sword and tried to angle her fire back at Bonny, but it merely bounced off her scales.

That was the thing about fake dragons, apparently – they had scales as strong as a real dragon, at the very least.

But even a real dragon had chinks in their armor – notably any orifices and the less-scaly underbelly. There, the scales were looser and thinner, and it was possible to get a sword in between them if it was shoved against the grain of the scales.

Blaze might not get so lucky, but he had to try.

He waited until she was close enough to reach him, then dropped to his knees, rolled and swung the sword.

Blood splattered down on him as Bonny shrieked. She caught his arm and chest with one of her back claws, but the damage to him was slight overall. Blaze rolled again and ended up behind Griff. He came to his feet and put his back to his bonded's, readying for another attack from Bonny.

Jade and Grlind were still alive and fighting, which relieved him. "Griff, are you —"

"I am unharmed," Griff said before chanting unfamiliar words.

Someone screamed, a long, drawn-out, agonized sound that would haunt Blaze.

Griff flapped his wings, and Blaze caught glimpses of Bonny circling in the distance. She seemed to be listing, and he realized she had one paw pressed to her gut.

Griff vibrated, and his body emitted heat as though he had his own fire inside.

Bonny turned and came at them with surprising speed, as if she'd never been injured moments before.

The air around Blaze and Griff crackled and popped with magic, and Blaze feared things were about to get much, much worse.

What happened was a complete surprise.

The sky itself seemed to rip open, and a battalion of dragons came through it, led by Fyre. Beside him was Artaxis, looking fierce as he pulled back the bowstring and let an arrow fly right at Xelscior.

Bonny growled, and Blaze knew this was it — she'd either kill him on this strike or die trying.

Griff and Xelscior lunged at each other.

Blaze wanted to help Griff but feared interfering would distract him instead. He held his ground as Bonny came at him, with Fyre chasing her.

Blaze waited until she was almost on him, then he shifted. There were many things he didn't want to do and letting Fyre kill his wife was a priority.

The sword fell to the ground, and Blaze thrust himself up. Bonny hadn't been prepared for such an attack. Blaze hit her in the chest and sent her sprawling fifty feet away, knocking down trees as she went.

He was on her before Fyre could reach her. *Why did you have to do this?* Blaze wished he could ask her. Instead, he had to dodge her claws and tail, her fire and teeth. Blaze slammed his head against hers, hoping to stun her. Whether it worked or not, he didn't know. He was lifted off her by a mighty gust of wind, and great bolts of lightning rained down on her.

Then Blaze flew of his own accord as he watched Bonny turn to ash. Jade nodded once, then wiped his hands together before looking at him.

Fyre landed beside Bonny's ashes and turned to look at Jade, then inclined his head in a way that conveyed thanks.

Blaze had to trust that Fyre wasn't going to harm Jade over Bonny's demise. He had to get to Griff's side and help him.

He turned and saw that Griff and Artaxis had Xelscior pinned between them. Xelscior was giving each of them his side, fighting off Artaxis's arrows and Griff's magic simultaneously.

Then Griff flicked his wrist, as if to say enough, and tipped his head up to the sky.

A vibrant swath of color, almost rainbow-like in form, arched down into Griff's palm and across from him, into Artaxis's hand as well.

The two men looked at each other, then Artaxis gave the slightest nod. As one, they each tossed the colorful magic, and it exploded over Xelscior, covering him.

Xelscior melted like snow tossed on a fire. It was disturbing to watch, yet Blaze couldn't look away as he lowered himself to the ground.

Then Griff was reaching for him, touching him, and Blaze had to curl himself around Griff, needed to be closer to him.

"Let me heal your wounds," Griff murmured, and Blaze basked in the love and care of his bonded.

Chapter Forty

Griff flapped his wings gently, moaning at the pleasure of having them back again.

Artaxis smiled at him. "Well, how did you find your wings?"

Blaze shifted, then stroked one of them. "They're beautiful."

"Stunning," Artaxis agreed. "Griff always did have the most incredible wings. That was part of the reason why I wanted him so badly."

Blaze growled, his top lip angling up in a sexy sneer.

Artaxis held his hands up. "I said *wanted*, dragon. I'd never poach on a bonded."

Griff was busy trying to calm Blaze down with subtle caresses. Distraction also seemed a good idea. "My wings weren't knocked off, per se. Xelscior took them from me."

"My father..." Artaxis shuddered. "He was always cruel, from what I remember of him. Not much of a Love fairy."

"He's my father too, unfortunately," Griff muttered. "And according to Ahndwa —"

"Your mother," Blaze pointed out.

Artaxis's eyes went wide. "You're a demigod, Griff?"

Griff blushed. "Well, I'm just me."

"A demigod," Blaze said proudly. "And *all mine!*"

"A demigod. Well, that explains a lot," Artaxis murmured.

Griff didn't think so. "Not really, but that's all I know besides that Xelscior wanted to kill me and take my soul because he sold his. There's no reincarnation for him. He's gone forever." Something Griff couldn't fathom. To never exist again? It was a terrifying thought. "My soul must be extra juicy or something for him to have wanted it so badly."

"It is a pure soul," said Ahndwa, appearing suddenly beside him.

Artaxis yelped and bowed down. "Goddess Ahndwa."

She touched Artaxis's nape. "Rise."

Artaxis did so gracefully. "Thank you."

Ahndwa nodded at him. "Griff's soul would have done more than give Xelscior more lives. It would have eradicated some of the evil that would have carried over into each of Xelscior's life. He sold his soul to the Underlord for power. It is obvious neither the Underlord nor Xelscior got a decent deal." She shrugged. "And the female, the one you called Bonny, she was one of the Underlord's concubines, sent to keep track of Xelscior."

"Bonny," Blaze said, turning to look toward where Fyre stood, staring down at some ashes and a burned spot on the ground. Jade and Grlind hovered behind

Fyre. "I should go over there and talk to him. He doesn't know."

"Perhaps give him a moment to grieve," Griff suggested.

Blaze nodded.

"He will recover and find his heart," Ahndwa said, "and I will return to speak with you again, my son."

Griff's heart fluttered a little at that. "Thank you."

Ahndwa brushed a kiss over his cheek, then was gone.

"That's amazing," Artaxis said. "I had no idea you were a demigod. When Shadnay came to get us, I imagined you and Blaze being in trouble some other way."

"Like what?" Griff asked.

Artaxis averted his gaze. "Er. Well, you know, with your memory issues, I guess I thought you might have gotten lost and ended up in a dangerous spot. Shadnay was quite insistent that we come help you. He just wasn't clear on the why of that, and he would *not* cease his buzzing until we'd gathered a sizable army to take with us."

Griff held out a hand and Shadnay buzzed right onto it. "Thank you, Shadnay."

Shadnay wiggled and flitted, then flew up to touch Griff's nose before darting off again.

"I think he has a crush," Artaxis observed.

Blaze only growled a little at that.

"Griff!" Gia shouted, appearing before him and lunging into a hug. "Oh my gods! You're still my brother, no matter what!"

Griff was trying to draw air into his lungs, but Gia was holding on to him so tight, it was difficult. He was squeezing her pretty tight in return.

"You heard?" he asked her a moment later.

Gia bobbed her head at him. "That my baby brother is a demigod? Oh yeah. I heard, *and* Ahndwa blessed me for helping to protect you." She beamed at him. "And don't think you get to boss me around just because you have her for your mother!"

"I wouldn't dream of it," Griff assured her. He purred a bit as Blaze caressed his wings again, but his pleasure dimmed when he spotted Fyre swiping at his cheeks. "Blaze? Should you — or we — go to Fyre?"

Blaze sighed. "Yeah, we should."

"Griff?"

Griff turned toward Jade. The Storm King didn't seem nearly as intimidating now that Griff knew his own lineage. That didn't mean he should be a dick. "Thank you, Jade, and you as well, Grlind, for helping us. Are either of you hurt?"

"Surprisingly, neither of us were harmed in this battle, unlike that with the fiends," Jade said. "But…but you *are* a demigod, and we *have* served you well and fought for you more than once."

Griff arched an eyebrow, trying to think what angle Jade was working. The fact was, both the elf and the orc had given selflessly of their time and risked their lives to aid him. "You're asking for a blessing?"

Jade cast his gaze down. "If it wouldn't be too much? I'd like to be able to return to my kingdom. I'm not asking for you to intervene in my battle, simply to — " He made a fluttering gesture around himself.

Griff looked at Grlind. "And you, orc? What would you ask for by way of a blessing?"

Grlind glanced at Jade quickly, then back at Griff. "Only that the Storm King is returned to his throne."

Jade frowned at Grlind. "No. You've already done enough. He needs an orc who will see the greatness in him and who will love him unconditionally."

Grlind was already shaking his head.

"An orc?" Griff asked. "Are you certain?"

Jade scowled at him. "Well, what else? Orcs only ever mate with their own kind."

"Better to go with the blessing I asked for," Grlind said. "I don't want what the Storm King is suggesting. It'd not be fair to have someone falling for me when I can't return their affections."

"What the hells does that mean?" Jade snapped, turning on Grlind. "You aren't capable of love? You don't deserve it? You—"

Grlind hung his head and muttered, "It means that my heart is already taken."

Jade shrank back as if he'd been slapped. "Oh. I see."

Griff was beginning to think that neither the elf nor the orc saw anything clearly. It wasn't his place to interfere, however, so he merely watched them for a moment before asking them if he could touch each of them as he murmured blessings over them.

The words should have seemed odd on his tongue, but they flowed as if he'd always known them. When he finished, he hugged them, his friends, even though he hadn't understood them to be such until then. Sometimes, he admitted silently, he was blind to what was before him.

But not to the love he had for Blaze. Griff cupped Blaze's jaw and kissed him, letting all his affection and gratitude flow into the kiss. Even though it was brief, he knew Blaze understood.

Then Griff took Blaze's hand in his. "Your brother?"

Blaze nodded.

Chapter Forty-One

Fyre looked broken. That was Blaze's first thought when he saw his brother. Tears streaked Fyre's cheeks, and his hands shook as he wiped at them.

But then Fyre raised his head and stared right at Blaze. The unmistakable fury in Fyre's eyes had the irises turning blue and orange with his inner fire.

Blaze hoped that anger wasn't about to be directed at him or his bonded. He moved to put himself between Fyre and Griff. "Fyre, I'm —"

"I can't *believe* she deceived me for so long!" Fyre raged, pounding his fists against his thighs. "How could I be so *stupid*? So *gullible*! Such a gods-be-damned *fool*! She lied to me with every fucking word she ever spoke, every touch she gave me, every fucking faked orgasm and promise of a family together and —" He threw his head back and bellowed, hot flames shooting from his mouth and nose. "I am so fucking mad at myself for being played by her!"

Blaze felt the heat rolling off his brother. He was afraid the man would combust if he didn't watch himself. "Fyre, you weren't a fool, aren't a fool for having believed in her. We all did. I did. I thought she was genuine." *Not always in a good way, either.* "Your kingdom believed in her and —"

"You believed, *they* believed, because I did," Fyre cut in, slashing angrily at the air as if he could slap away Blaze's words. "And I fell for her lies because I'm a fucking fool!"

Blaze opened his mouth to argue, but Fyre didn't give him a chance.

"This is proof of my idiocy," he said, nodding at the ashes. "My failure as king, my failure as a man and brother, a son. As anything. You." He pointed to Blaze.

"Me?" Blaze repeated, confused and scared of what was coming.

Fyre nodded. "Yes, you and your demigod bonded, I give my kingdom to you both to rule. You'll do better by far than I ever could."

Blaze panicked. "I don't want to be king!"

But Fyre had shifted and was already flapping away. He didn't even acknowledge Blaze's refusal.

"Fyre!" Blaze shouted. "You get back here! *Get back here!* I don't want to be king! Or queen! Or whatever! Gods damn it!"

"I don't think he's in any place to listen right now," Griff said. "Let him have some time to himself, time to heal and see the truth. He'll come to understand that it wasn't him but Bonny who was in the wrong. I hope."

Blaze wanted to go after Fyre. It hurt to know his brother was in so much pain. Fyre wouldn't thank Blaze for it if he did pursue him, though. Fyre had as much pride as any other dragon, more, even, and it'd been decimated by Bonny. Only time would help him now. Blaze had to trust in his brother's ability to reason.

It still felt wrong to let him go. Blaze was going to have to step back, however. It was what he and Fyre both needed.

Even so, he wanted some comfort, and Griff was frowning. Sliding his hand over Griff's silky wings helped soothe them both.

Griff made the sweetest purring sounds when Blaze did it.

"I think I'm going to be touching these a lot," Blaze said, smiling at Griff. "In fact, I can't wait to see what you do with them when we're making love."

Griff wasn't slow at all. He smiled wickedly. "Well then, let's go home and find out."

But nothing was that easy. There were congratulations to be accepted by fairies and dragons, and Blaze's mind was blown by the dragons that kneeled for him in a show of respect—and he nearly tripped to see Bort doing so.

Blaze stopped walking and looked down at him.

Bort smirked, though there was a nervous edge to it. "I know, right? Weird. But here's the thing—I can admit I was a dick. You're obviously a man blessed by the gods, and I'm not stupid all the time. I'd rather curry your favor than your wrath now."

Blaze wasn't sure that was the best promise to follow him, but it was an honest one, so he'd take it. "So this is a truce."

"A permanent one," Bort agreed. "And I won't let anyone else insult my king."

Blaze felt as though he'd fallen through space onto another planet. "Uh. Okay. Thanks. I mean, blessings to you and your family."

Bort snickered. "I'll help you study up on kingly behavior."

"He doesn't need the help," Griff said. "Blaze is perfect just as he is."

Bort tucked his chin down. "I didn't mean anything bad by it."

Griff touched Bort's head, right on top. "I know, but he must rule as he is, not as anyone thinks he should be. Blaze is at his best all the time, but especially when he allows his heart to guide him instead of worrying over other people's opinions."

Blaze couldn't help it. He had responsibilities he'd never imagined, a kingdom suddenly depending on him, subjects needing reassurances, but he had to pull Griff into his arms. "Thank you for believing in me. I love you, so much."

Griff's smile was brighter than any dragon's flame. "I love you, too."

Epilogue

"A king and a demigod. This world is about to be shaken," Jade teased. "Just try not to take over my kingdom, please, if you decide on total planetary domination. Let me keep my little corner of it."

Griff rolled his eyes but couldn't keep back a grin. "Fine. If we must."

"You are too kind." Jade bowed with a flourish. "I suppose I must get back to my battle now. It's been...different."

"Prick," Blaze muttered. He snickered when Jade gave him an innocent look. "You know you are."

"It's because I'm royalty, and I'm fairly certain *someone* here made comments about royalty being screwed-up and haughty. Oh wait." Jade blinked.

Blaze groaned and covered his face with both hands. "Don't remind me! But I'm not *king*-king, just a temporary filler."

"You're still a king," Jade informed him. "And I think you might be one for longer than you expect."

"Why do you say that?" Blaze asked, though he didn't give Jade the chance to answer. "Fyre is strong, and he's made to be a ruler. He'll be back soon. He'll get past what Bonny did to him."

Jade shook his head. "It's not what she did to him that haunts him, but what he sees as his own failures." He turned when Grlind called out that he was ready. "Ah. I wish you both well in life."

Griff had kept his distance from the Storm King all along, but thought it was time to let go of the distrust he'd felt for the elf.

He wasn't expecting the hug from Jade, though. "Uh?"

Jade giggled and squeezed him. "Oh, come on. You're as close to a god as I'll ever get to touch."

"You've touched him plenty," Blaze grumbled, though he sounded more amused than irritated.

Jade released Griff and lunged for Blaze. "Jealous? Here's your hug, hottie."

"No—aw, shit," Blaze whined, but patted Jade on the back. "Okay, now, fine, get off of me."

Jade did, and that left only Grlind to say goodbye to. However, the orc stayed back, shaking his head.

"Don't care much for goodbyes," Grlind said. "Safe journey to you."

"Safe journey to you as well," Griff replied.

"If we can ever be of any help, or you just want to visit, you'll always be welcome," Blaze added, taking hold of Griff's hand. They watched the Storm King and the orc walk away. "Why do I feel like crying?"

Griff turned to Blaze. "Because they were better friends than we realized until this moment."

"I was always suspicious of them, well, mainly of Jade," Blaze admitted.

Griff wasn't certain that Jade was as selfless as he portrayed himself to be. He had wondered, and maybe still did, if Jade had somehow known of Griff's semi-divinity.

"I suppose you'll be living with the dragons?"

Griff glanced at Artaxis. "For a while, yes, but we'll be heading to my house first. I have to get Egregio."

"That's your pet, right?" Blaze asked.

"Yes, though don't let him hear you say that. Egregio will take your toes off," Griff warned. "As far as Egregio is concerned, I'm the pet, and you will be, too."

Blaze scowled. "Why would you want a mean pet?"

"Because he's really cuddly and soft and warm," Griff explained.

Artaxis just laughed at them both and promised to meet them at the frolic.

Blaze had to deal with his army of dragons before Griff was finally able to have Blaze all to himself. He turned his face up to the sky, squinting against the suns' bright rays.

"Ready to fly with me?"

Griff spread his wings. "Always."

Flying with Blaze was unlike anything Griff had ever experienced before. It was fun and sensual, an erotic dance between the two of them at times. When they landed at his house, Griff's entire body was vibrating with the need to touch Blaze's naked skin and to mate with his bonded.

But as soon as he tugged Blaze inside, Egregio yowled and leapt on Blaze's foot, biting at his toes.

"Ow! Shit! *OW!* You evil little shit!" Blaze yelled, hopping on his other foot. "Get it off me! I'm gonna toast your fuzzy ass—"

"Egregio, behave," Griff said, then cooed, and Egregio sprang up into his arms.

Blaze glared daggers at the beast. "*That* is evil incarnate."

Griff scratched behind Egregio's ear. "Be nice."

"It attacked me!" Blaze shouted.

Egregio growled.

"And he'll do it again if you continue to yell." Griff peered past Egregio to Blaze's foot. "He didn't break the skin."

"It still hurt." Blaze's bottom lip poked out as he pouted.

Griff gave Egregio one last scratch. "Go on, and be good. No more attacking my bonded."

Egregio leapt down and made an inquisitive sound.

"Yes, he's my bonded, my lovely dragon, Blaze, and he's a king. Keep that in mind the next time you go into attack mode." Griff chuckled as Egregio puffed up, then skittered under the bed.

Blaze squatted and poked at his foot. "We're not having sex on the bed, right?"

Griff waggled his eyebrows, then stood in front of Blaze, his cock nearly eye level with the sexy dragon.

Blaze was looking up at him, lips parted, eyes dark with lust.

"Right here works," Griff rasped. He took hold of his hardening cock and brushed the tip of it over Blaze's lips. "Keep your hands behind your back," he ordered when Blaze started to reach for him. "Or on my thighs if you need the support."

"Need to touch you," Blaze muttered, his palms warm on Griff's legs.

"You'll get to touch." But for now, Griff had a need to see his cock slipping into Blaze's mouth. "Open for me."

Blaze did so after licking his lips, slicking the way for Griff's shaft to glide over them.

Griff let go of his cock and instead held on to Blaze, one hand at his nape, the other cupping his jaw. "Yes," he hissed, sinking into the pleasure of Blaze's mouth instantly. "Fuck. Take me deeper."

Blaze's nostrils flared, and little clouds of steam gusted from them. He bobbed his head down, and Griff's eyes crossed as silky wet perfection encased his length.

"Oh," he whispered, his knees going weak as Blaze swallowed and moaned. "Gods."

Blaze moaned again and slurped his way back to the tip, where he tongued and teased at Griff's slit.

Griff was panting, and his legs were shaking in minutes, his balls drawn tight as he struggled to keep from coming just yet.

He let himself fuck Blaze's mouth a few more times, then pulled back and rubbed his cock on Blaze's cheeks, the rough scrape of stubble almost more than Griff could bear. Almost. But not quite. The little bite of pain added to the arousal coursing through Griff.

"Can I?" Blaze asked, his voice raspy from sucking Griff.

"Go ahead. Don't make me come." Griff let Blaze take hold of his cock and worship it, with tongue and lips and caresses.

All the while, Blaze spoke to him of love and devotion, and Griff promised him an eternity together.

Nothing would keep them apart. Not enemies, not pride, not death.

Griff pulled Blaze to his feet and kissed his swollen lips. He held Blaze in his arms, touching his hot skin and stroking over firm muscles.

"Griff, please. I need you." Blaze trembled as Griff sucked up a purple mark above his collarbone. "Griff!"

Pleased with the way Blaze was unraveling for him, Griff walked Blaze backward, then laid him out on the table. He followed Blaze down, kissing him until they had to separate for breath. Griff nibbled his way down to Blaze's nipples, where he proceeded to work them into stiff peaks as Blaze writhed beneath him.

Griff left marks down Blaze's chest to his taut belly, then in the divot where groin and leg met. Blaze squirmed and giggled at first, then scrambled for a hold of the table and brought his heels up to the surface of it, offering himself to Griff.

Griff licked Blaze's cock from shaft to base, then came up and took half the length into his mouth while at the same time palming Blaze's balls.

"Argh!" Blaze jolted, hips shooting up and cock sinking deep.

Griff's eyes watered as he relaxed his throat muscles rather than stiffening up at the sudden thrust. He tugged Blaze's balls gently, then slid his hand down to rub over Blaze's taint.

Blaze mewled and rutted, and Griff let him, giving Blaze this, the control to take what he needed.

Blaze buried his fingers in Griff's hair and began to move with more purpose, losing himself to the bliss Griff could give him.

Then Blaze keened and jerked away, twisting his hips and pulling his cock from Griff's mouth.

"In me," Blaze demanded, panting heavily, still lying halfway on his side. "I want you in me!"

Like Griff would ever argue with that. "Let me get the lube."

"Hurry," Blaze pleaded.

Griff had never moved so fast in his life. He had the lube open and spread on his cock in less than ten seconds. But when he would have used his fingers to prepare Blaze, Blaze shook his head.

"No. Just your cock. I want you to fill me like that," he said, pulling his legs up and baring himself to Griff.

Griff's heart pounded as he lined up his tip to that little hole. "You'll tell me if it's too much."

Blaze rolled his eyes. "I'm fixing to tell you to hurry the—oh—" This time his eyes rolled for a different reason.

Griff grinned as he pressed into Blaze, slowly breaching his hole with a steady pressure.

The perfect grip of Blaze's body was mind-boggling. Griff's smug grin slipped away as he struggled for restraint.

Blaze's ass was so hot, the temperature of his inner fire evident in every rippling clench of his anal walls. They pulled Griff's shaft in deeper, massaging it and working every inch of it.

Griff lifted one knee onto the table as he pushed the rest of the way into Blaze's ass. He had to close his eyes and start naming off species of plants to keep from coming right then.

Blaze's ass clenched, then finally, he grunted and Griff could move.

"Gods, Blaze," Griff got out before he withdrew almost fully. The underside of his cockhead stretched Blaze's rim beautifully. "You should see—" He thrust back in, hard.

Blaze gasped, his body arching as he grabbed onto Griff's arms.

Griff couldn't hold back any longer. He gritted out Blaze's name as he took his bonded and gave of himself in return.

Griff pounded into Blaze, pushing him across the table so that Griff had to climb up onto it and hold Blaze. It was no hardship. He wanted to hold Blaze forever, and he would.

He kissed Blaze, a messy, more teeth than lips kiss as they clung to each other, Blaze driving his hips up eagerly in time with Griff's movements.

Never enough. Griff would never get enough of Blaze. He moaned and thrust faster. He was too close to climaxing.

He tried to get a hand between their bodies, but Blaze beat him to it, fisting his own cock. Griff instead pinched one of Blaze's nipples. He managed to get out one word. "Come."

Blaze gasped, and his dick sprayed hot cum between them.

Griff's orgasm tore through him like a summer storm, violent and perfect. He shouted, his body suffused with a pleasure so intense he couldn't do anything but feel.

Aftershocks of it kept rippling through him for several seconds before he lowered himself gracelessly to Blaze's side, rolling Blaze with him.

He had many words to say, later. Right now, they were in a perfect place — each other's arms, and only three words needed to be said on his part. "I love you."

Blaze sniffled. "And I love you."

Griff smiled and held his bonded closer, brushing a tender kiss over his cheek. He was sure they'd have many more adventures in the future, but for now, he couldn't imagine a more perfect moment than the one he was sharing with Blaze.

Want to see more from this author?
Here's a taster for you to enjoy!

Wild Ones: Destined Prey
Bailey Bradford

Excerpt

Jack Tucker watched his brother retrieve the rifle from the gun cabinet in the office. "Um. Rhett? What're you doing?"

Rhett didn't even glance back at him as he loaded the gun. "What does it look like I'm doing? You been living in the city so long you forgot how a Wyoming rancher lives?" Then he *did* look over his shoulder at Jack, and Jack kind of wished he hadn't.

He hated seeing that judgment in his brother's eyes, and knowing he'd never be good enough for Rhett, never be the man Rhett was. "No," Jack mumbled, "I didn't forget."

Rhett sighed and turned until he faced Jack. "Look, that was uncalled for. I'm… I'm sorry, okay?"

Jack was so startled by the apology that he gulped and couldn't think of a word to say.

Rhett grimaced. "Yeah. Well, okay. Gotta check on some tracks Eddie said he found leading from his property to ours. I'll be back in a few hours." He left, striding from the room without seeming to hesitate.

Jack groaned and closed his eyes. Of course Rhett didn't hesitate—he never had. Rhett always knew what to do, and how to do it, and who he was and that he was right… *Except, he apologized to me, and it screwed my head right up.*

"Worse than it already is," he muttered. Jack couldn't stop himself from touching his left side, where his bruised ribs throbbed as the pain meds wore off. He was lucky, very lucky, that Rhett hadn't pushed him on the *accident* that had sent Jack running home from New York, and possibly into the unemployment line. His boss hadn't been happy with Jack taking off, even with a medical note as an excuse. Jack hadn't told Rhett much about any of that. As far as Rhett knew, Jack had fallen down some icy steps, and that was all he was going to ever know about the incident.

Jack replayed his brother's apology in his head and somehow it mingled in with Alex's. Cold fear trickled down Jack's spine and his gut cramped hard enough to make him worry about the dinner he'd just eaten.

After several minutes of trying to calm himself down, Jack stood and left. He'd wanted to sit and talk with Rhett about finances and try to decide if he should offer to let Rhett buy him out. Jack wasn't made to be a rancher. He wasn't made to be a New Yorker, either.

Jack didn't know what he was supposed to do in life, and at the age of twenty-seven, he kind of thought he should have an inkling.

His cell phone rang as he stepped into his bedroom. Without looking, he knew it was Alex calling. "Who else would it be?" he huffed. It wasn't like he had any friends left.

Rather than check to see how many times Alex had called and how many texts he'd sent, Jack turned the phone off, then stuck it in the nightstand. He eased himself onto the bed, then took a couple of pain pills and washed them down with the rest of the water he'd brought in earlier.

The glass was old and familiar, and he felt a pang of regret as he looked it over after he set it down. Green glass, nothing special about it, yet it brought back so many memories.

He could see his mom in the kitchen, fixing a pitcher of tea, talking to him and listening as he told her about his day at school or the chores he'd had to do around the ranch. She'd always been so kind and understanding that Jack had to believe she'd have been fine about him being gay. He'd spent many afternoons in the kitchen, helping her prepare meals or just basking in her presence. Losing her had almost broken him.

For a few more minutes, he let his mind go back to happy childhood days. His dad wasn't in nearly as many of those good memories, but Chauncey Tucker hadn't been a bad man. His dad had been more like Rhett—stoic, focused on the ranch and less on the people around him.

Jack ran one finger around the rim of the glass. He was surprised, really, that there were any of the old things left.

The sound of gunshot startled him so badly he jerked and nearly sent the glass flying.

"Shit!" He winced, then stood as quickly as he could manage.

Another shot rang out, then a third, and fear quickly overtook every other sensation he'd felt until then.

Rhett had always been an ace shot. If he'd had to use three bullets, then there was something bad outside—a bear or a whole pack of wolves.

Jack didn't like guns, but he went and got one from the gun cabinet anyway. He loaded it as he walked to the front door, and hoped like hell Rhett wasn't hurt.

As soon as he stepped outside, the fine hairs at his nape seemed to stand up and vibrate, like some kind of primitive survival instinct. Jack froze, his back to the door and his heart slamming hard against his ribs.

Another shot sounded, and it jolted Jack into action. "Rhett! Rhett!" He rushed down the steps and toward the direction the shots had come from. "Rhett! Are you okay?"

When Rhett didn't immediately answer, Jack ran, aware that he was being careless with his gun but had all his attention on finding his brother as soon as possible.

"Rhett!" He stumbled over something on the ground and almost fell before he managed to flail enough to keep himself upright.

Pain tore down his injured side, but he ignored it, calling out for his brother yet again. He cursed himself for not thinking to grab a flashlight. The sky was overcast and there was no moonlight to assist him in his search, and once he was past the barns there was no light coming from the house or other structures, either.

The cattle in the closest field were making enough noise to drown out his voice or Rhett's, making it impossible for them to hear each other — the sounds of the gunshots must have scared them. Jack worried about a stampede, but he'd never seen any of the critters take out a fence, so he dismissed the idea.

"Rhett!" His throat burned as he hollered again.

Lightning streaked across the sky, blinding Jack for a moment, then thunder followed and he couldn't contain his startled yelp as his ears rang from the sound.

Or his shriek when six pairs of glowing yellow eyes appeared between him and the fence line.

"Shit!" Jack skidded to a halt, hoping he could steady his hands, and force himself to do what he had to do.

PUBLISHING

Sign up for our newsletter and find out about all our romance book releases, eBook sales and promotions, sneak peeks and FREE romance books!

About the Author

A native Texan, Bailey spends her days spinning stories around in her head, which has contributed to more than one incident of tripping over her own feet. Evenings are reserved for pounding away at the keyboard, as are early morning hours. Sleep? Doesn't happen much. Writing is too much fun, and there are too many characters bouncing about, tapping on Bailey's brain demanding to be let out.

Caffeine and chocolate are permanent fixtures in Bailey's office and are never far from hand at any given time. Removing either of those necessities from Bailey's presence can result in what is known as A Very, Very Scary Bailey and is not advised under any circumstances.

Bailey loves to hear from readers. You can find her contact information, website details and author profile page at https://www.pride-publishing.com